THE GATEKEEPER AND THE WATCHER

Den JR Hedges

Published in the United Kingdom by Self Publishing by the author.

First Published in the United Kingdom in 2017 by the author
First edition

To my wife, Jane, thank you for all your support.

Chapter One

The little girl tugged at the kitchen chair again, trying to move it another few inches. She managed to move it a little but one of the legs soon became stuck in a tear in the lino. It had worn thin where the chair was constantly pulled in and out from the table without being lifted and the lack of care meant that the linoleum had cracked and torn in several places. Tug as she might, she couldn't move it any further. She sniffed back her tears, a few whimpers escaping in spite of her best efforts to be strong and brave.

She was so hungry—and cold.

She'd hoped to be able to climb up onto the chair so she could reach the cupboards and see if she could find herself something to eat but at only four-years-old, small, and skinny for her age, even the wooden chair felt as if it were made of lead. She hadn't eaten a decent meal in what her tummy was saying was forever. Her stomach alternated between feeling like a hard, painful knot and an aching, hollow pit. It looked as if she wasn't going to eat again today.

The only thing she was tall enough to actually reach in the kitchen was the bottom door of the fridge freezer, and luckily for her, that was the freezer section. In her house, the freezer was never full of goodies such as ice cream or frozen yoghurt, or anything else nice that was meant to be eaten still frozen or without any cooking. In fact, there wasn't much in there at all except the microwave dinners that were the only thing her daddy seemed to eat. The best she'd found had been a bag of frozen peas, probably left over from the days when she used to have a mommy who cooked. She'd taken them out and was hoping that they'd thaw out quickly, but the house was almost as cold as the inside of the freezer itself. Daddy only ever puts the heating on when he was at home, and he wasn't home a lot. She was so hungry she'd considered eating them anyway, but she knew that they would only give her a very sore tummy. She would have to wait and hope that they didn't take more than a day or two to thaw out, or that her father would actually remember to feed her before then. That reminded her, she'd better hide them in her room or he would take them away from her.

She was on her way out of the kitchen when she suddenly thought about the chair. She'd managed to move it a little way before it had gotten stuck. She'd better see if she could move it back into place at the table or else he might notice. If he noticed, then things would be very, very bad indeed.

He wasn't normally really mean when he came home from work, as long as she'd stayed in her room for most of the day like a good girl and not touched anything anywhere else in the house. She was supposed to only go from her room to the bathroom and back again. Coming downstairs was strictly off limits and she would be in big trouble if he knew that she had. She definitely wouldn't get any supper and he would probably lock her in her room straight away instead of waiting until he was ready to go back out again. That would mean she wouldn't have any time to sit in the living room by the living flame fire with him and watch the television he would turn on while he sat in the armchair and ate his microwave dinner. Those moments were precious to her, especially in the winter when it was the only time she ever felt warm and cosy.

With all this in mind, she desperately tried to move the chair back to where she'd found it, but it refused to move in any direction. She finally worked out that she needed to lift the leg that was stuck out of the hole before she could slide it, but by that time, she was too weak and too tired. She gave it everything she had but she couldn't lift and move at the same time. In the end, she gave up, grabbed her bag of peas, and ran back to her room, hoping against hope that Daddy didn't give the chair, not quite being under the table as it was, a moment's thought.

Once back in her room and with the peas hidden as far under her bed as she could reach, she accepted that her mission had been a failure. She allowed herself to give in to the abject misery of that fact, even though she didn't deserve to feel sorry for herself. She didn't deserve anything. Her daddy told her that all the time. According to him, it had been her fault Mummy had left so she deserved all the bad things that happened to her afterwards. He left her in no doubt of that.

She didn't know how long Mummy had been gone for but she did remember her. Some of the memories flashed through her head now. A smiling face close to her own as yummy food was spooned into her mouth, being cuddled in a warm towel and gentle arms after a hot bath, being tickled before getting tucked in at night, a soft voice reading to her or telling her stories, and sweet kisses goodnight. It seemed to her like everything had been better when Mummy was here. Even Daddy was happy then. She could remember the sound of him laughing, could remember what his face looked like when he was smiling, could remember being lifted in his arms and spun around, or sat up on his shoulders so she felt like a queen looking down on her kingdom. What she remembered most of all was feeling happy and loved back then, but Daddy said that Mummy had never loved her so she must be wrong. In fact, he said she'd hated her and that was why she left. It was all her fault.

This time, she did allow the tears to come.

***

She tensed when she heard his car in the driveway, flinched when she heard him slamming the car door, and cringed as she heard him turn his key in the lock and step inside. *Please don't notice the chair, please don't notice the chair*, she chanted over and over in her mind.

Earlier, once she'd cried until her throat hurt and no more tears would come, she'd gone into the bathroom and splashed her face with cold water from the bath tap. She couldn't reach the sink yet, but she needed to wash away the evidence of her sobbing spree. If he saw her red and puffy eyes, he would be angry with her. He hated when she cried. He would call her a pathetic little cry baby, a wimp, or a sissy. She really disliked those names; they made her feel weak and ashamed. Mostly, she tried never to cry but sometimes she just couldn't help it. After she'd washed away the evidence of her misery, she'd gone back to her room and picked up one of her books. The only books she had were the ones her mother had bought to read to her. She couldn't actually read them but by looking at the pictures she could recall her mother's voice telling the story, and how much they'd giggled together as she'd put on different voices for different characters. Often, looking at them would make her happy, but not today. Today the book just left her with an even bigger empty pit of longing in her tight stomach. She'd sat very still and stared at the page, although she wasn't really seeing it anymore.

She realised she must have been sitting there for ages when she heard her father returning from work. This was the moment when she'd find out if she'd managed to ruin the one and only time she ever felt anything close to happiness.

She listened to him throw his keys into the bowl on the unit in the hallway, then walk into the living room. She knew he'd be shrugging off his jacket and tossing it over the back of the sofa, then turning on the fire and the television. After that, he would come upstairs to change out of his work clothes. Once he'd done that was usually when she found out if he'd had a *good* day or a *bad* day.

She didn't know what those terms really meant for him, didn't even know what her daddy did for work, but she knew the different outcomes for her. On some nights, he would pop his head into her room and tell her he'd had a good day and she should come down for dinner. Those were the best nights. On other nights, it would be as if he'd forgotten she was there and he wouldn't speak to her at all at this stage. She knew that those were bad days. The very worst days were when he came into the house and was already muttering angrily. Those were the days that she would fervently hope that he would forget all about her, but he never did on those types of days.

Today must have been a good day.

"Candy, come downstairs for dinner!" he yelled.

Normally, she would have thanked him and leapt to her feet to race downstairs; taking her place on the floor by the fire, drinking in what was being shown on TV. It was normally a stuffy, boring program that he called the news but she didn't care. It was other people, it was the outside world, and it fascinated her. She didn't often understand what it was they were talking about as they used big words she'd never heard, but it was so wonderful to simply hear another voice. Candy didn't have any interaction with other people, not since her mother had left. Tonight, she was slow to rise and hesitant and she made her way to her bedroom door. He hadn't been in the kitchen yet. If she were already downstairs when he found the chair, it would probably make things worse. Therefore, she took her time, dragging her feet, wondering what excuse she could come up with to slow her down even more. Suddenly, she thought of it.

"Daddy, may I go to the bathroom first, please?"

Already on his way downstairs and a few steps from the top, he glanced back at her impatiently. "Candy, you're not a baby anymore. If you need to go, then go."

"Thank you."

She scarpered. Once there, she pushed the door mostly closed but left it open a tiny crack, putting her little ear to it to listen to his feet pounding down the rest of the stairs. She heard movement in the kitchen, drawers opening, the rattle of cutlery, the slam of a door, and the sound of the microwave being turned on. None of it sounded excessively angry. Maybe he hadn't thought anything of the moved chair, maybe thought that was where he'd left it in his rush to leave this morning. Maybe, just maybe, she would get away with it. When she heard the microwave beep and then start up again she dared to hope for even more than that. Mind you, she'd been caught out that way before, thinking she was going to be fed, then realising that it was only Daddy's meal going back in for more cooking. She knew she had to go downstairs and find out one way or another.

Her feet were leaden as she descended the steps. She practically crept into the kitchen, quiet as a mouse, afraid even to breathe too loudly. Her father was sitting at the kitchen table, examining the instructions on the cardboard sleeve that he'd removed from the plastic container of food.

"There you are," he said, noticing her in spite of her stealth. "I don't suppose this will be any good but it'll fill a gap, eh?"

Candy's face broke into a beaming smile. Daddy was talking to her! He'd had a good day, didn't know she was the one that had moved the chair, and now they were going to have dinner together. She wouldn't have to eat the peas while they were cold and hard. This was a very good day for her too!

"Can I help with anything, Daddy?"

He shook his head. "You'll only drop something, spill something, or break something."

Candy knew it was true. She was often clumsy around her father, but it was only because she was always so nervous around him that her hands trembled. She couldn't think of being clumsy at any other time. She nodded, agreeing with him.

"Go and sit in the living room. I'll bring this through when it's ready."

She didn't need to be told twice. Happily, she ran through to the living room and sat on the floor by the fire, drinking in the warmth, listening to the voices on the TV, and seeing the images of other places flash up for brief moments. She would have been more comfortable on the sofa or one of the chairs, but Daddy didn't like her up there with food in case she spilled something. She had before and he'd made her clean it up, but she'd done such a bad job he'd had to take over himself. That had ended with her being sent to her room without being allowed to finish her dinner, so she wasn't going to complain about sitting on the floor—not when she was about to receive a hot meal and be allowed to sit with him for a while. Maybe he would even talk to her some more.

Chapter Two

Candy was back in her room, this time with the door locked. This was the very worst part of her day. Daddy never stayed home for long. After he'd eaten and tidied up, throwing out the empty containers and washing up the forks, it was time for Candy to go back upstairs and get ready for bed. He would stand over her while she got changed into her pyjamas, make her use the bathroom one last time and brush her teeth at the sink, standing on a step stool that he would take down from the high windowsill to allow her to reach. Then she would wash her face and he would walk behind her as she went into her room and climbed into bed. There were no bedtime stories or goodnight kisses; he didn't even tuck her in. Instead, he would stand by the door until he was satisfied that she was settled.

"Remember, no getting out of bed, no turning on the light, and keep away from the window."

Candy would nod, well rehearsed in her night time instructions, similar to the day ones except he took no chances at night. He'd told her once that if anyone saw her alone in the house through the day, he could probably explain it away with her being too sick to go to her child minder and he had to go to work, but if anyone saw her alone in the house at night, then they would be angry with him and take her away from him. Candy didn't want that for reasons she didn't really understand. From her flashes of memories of her mother and father when she littler, she knew that her life should be different but she wasn't sure how. With her limited experience, she didn't know that her father wasn't a good man and shouldn't be responsible for the care of a four-year-old girl. She didn't know that her childhood should be filled with love, friends, happiness, play, and laughter. All she knew was that Daddy was the only family she had and she didn't want anyone taking her away, so she would obey all the orders he gave her and hide if the doorbell rang and never be tempted to peak, stay away from the windows and not make too much noise, never answer the telephone, and not to wander all over the house where she might be seen from outside.

Once Candy was tucked into bed with the blankets pulled up to her chin, he nodded and left the room. She watched the door close behind him and heard the key turn in the lock. As soon as she heard the front door slam, the hard knot in her stomach returned. At nights, Daddy went to someplace he called 'the pub'. She didn't know what it was but she thought that it must be a very bad place indeed. When her Daddy came home from this place, it was as if he'd always had a *bad* day. She couldn't understand why he kept on going. He was always unsteady on feet, swaying and staggering, he smelled ready bad, like stale and bitter things, and he was always, always very angry. This was the one time when he never forgot about Candy. When he came home from 'the pub', he always sought her out, and it was never for a good reason. That's why her fear began the moment he left and would only get worse and worse as she waited for him to return.

When Daddy came home from this horrible place, he would take all his anger out on her, would rant and rave about how unfair everything was, and how much he hated looking at her face that reminded him so much of her mother's. He would use his fists as well as his voice to put her into a place of such pain and terror that her small vocabulary just didn't have the words to express. She didn't know what was worse, the pain she felt on her body or the pain she felt in her heart.

With no way to tell how much time had passed, Candy didn't stay in bed for too long. There was no way she could sleep during this period of building trepidation, and her bed was a place of comfort and sanctuary that she scrambled into after the terrible time was over. She wanted to keep it that way and if she lay there growing more and more afraid, it would lose that power to soothe her and make her feel safe. She climbed out and went to crouch in the corner, hugging her knees and gently rocking back and forth. She hummed tunelessly, zoning out. It was the familiar press on her bladder that brought her back to reality and made her aware that some time had passed since her father had left. This only worried her even more. With the door locked, there was no way she could get to the bathroom.

She'd once wet the bed when she was smaller and received such a beating that she'd barely been able to move for what felt like weeks and weeks. She hadn't made that mistake again, but she was too small to be able to hold it for the length of time that he was away. Sobbing her heart out with shame and discomfort after her accidents on the floor, she'd begged and begged him to leave her a bucket or basin but he'd refused, saying she had to grow up and learn. She'd often be sitting in a puddle of her own urine when he returned. As she got older, her bladder got bigger and stronger, but it would always be fit to explode by the time he arrived home. Tonight was no different.

Her fear reached fever pitch as she heard the front door open and her father's footsteps on the stairs. Her bedroom door burst open and in the landing light behind him, he was nothing more than a huge silhouette, a terrifying figure of darkness inside and out.

Then he flipped on her light and what she saw was even worse.

His face was a mix of purples and reds, blotchy from nose to cheeks. His mouth was twisted into a mocking sneer and the eyes were bulging as they stared at her, a look of pure hatred on his face. She could smell that reek of bitterness and staleness. She knew what was coming, knew exactly what to expect. Her overstretched bladder let go, a warm stream of urine soaking through her pyjamas and running down her leg. She began to tremble and shake. The sight of her infuriated him even more and he burst into a rant that rapidly became a tirade of vile curse words and abuse.

Candy wanted to run but was frozen to the spot. Even if she could have moved, there was nowhere to run to and it would only make things worse when he finally caught up with her. She knew that from bitter experience. She'd only tried it once and would never try it again. Instead, she stood there, her skinny legs and feet soaked, her head bowed, trying to hide the face he hated because it reminded him too much of her mother. She still saw the fists ball at his sides, saw those first few lurching steps towards her. An arm was raised as he found his unsteady stride and she screwed up her face against the impact that she knew was about to land on her body. At the last minute, she raised her head, wanting to judge where it might land so she could try and brace herself and maybe this time prevent the blow from sending her flying across the room. Besides, it was better when it didn't come as a surprise. What she saw made her open her mouth to scream, but no sound came out.

A figure was entering her room behind her father, moving at speed.

Candy didn't know what was happening. Nothing like this had ever happened before. She sort of remembered outside from when her mother was around and she vaguely remembered other people from that time too, but no one had come to their house since the day she'd gone. Were they here to hurt her and be bad to her too? Those were the only thoughts that had time to form in her small mind and from then on, she could only watch events unfold.

The figure stepped up behind her father with a grace Candy had never seen before, but there looked nothing gentle about the way it grabbed the arm that was raised to strike her and yanked it down before twisting it hard behind his back. Her father's eyes, already bulging with rage and intent, went wider still and Candy wondered if they were going to pop right out of his head. Whether they might have done or not, she would never know as the figure leant forward and whispered something close to her father's ear, so low that there was no chance of her hearing what was said. The person then raised its other hand and touched him on the right shoulder with two fingers. Candy looked on in shock as her dad fell to the floor and immediately curled up into a ball and began to cry. She was more scared than she'd ever been in her life. At least with her father, she knew exactly how much horror and pain she would be subjected to, she knew the routine and could usually tell when it would start and when it would end. This was something completely different.

The figure stepped over her father and moved towards Candy, giving her no chance to run as it swept her up into its arms. She began to scream. She tried to struggle but was helpless within those strong arms and no matter how much she tried to twist and wriggle, kick, hit, and scratch, it made no difference. Her captor simply turned her around and shunted her a little higher in their arms as they stepped over her father and headed for the door.

"Daddy! Daddy! Help me!"

Her cries were frantic, her face tear-streaked as her little arms reached back over the shoulder of her abductor towards her father. "Don't let them take me away, Daddy!"

Her father didn't even acknowledge her.

CHAPTER THREE

When Candy woke up, she couldn't quite figure out where she was. The bed felt soft and warm, a fluffy duvet almost weightless on top of her. She raised her head that was resting across her arm and found she was no longer wearing her own pyjamas but a flannel nightgown that was adding to the whole cosy feel of everything around her. Then she remembered. Once more, she began to scream, but this time, she wasn't ignored.

A tall woman came hurrying into her room, sitting down on the bed and wrapping her arms around her. "It's okay, Candy, you're all right, everything's going to be okay," she soothed in a gentle voice.

"I want my Daddy," Candy wailed, seeking the only bit of familiarity and constant she had in her life.

"There, just cry, get it all out. You must have had a shock, I know, but things will be okay, you'll see soon."

Feeling the arms around her, Candy realised they felt familiar to her. "It was you! You hurt my Daddy."

She squirmed free and began to pound her tiny fists against the woman's chest. "I hate you, I hate you. Take me home! I want my Daddy. What did you do to him? You're a nasty, horrible, mean lady and I'm going to call the police. I want to go home."

The woman looked sad for a moment, then she gave Candy a reassuring smile. "Your Daddy is absolutely fine, dear. He's gone to work this morning as always. You will have to trust me on that as you can't see him right now. You will understand a bit later, I promise. I know this is all very scary and different for you, but we'll talk properly later. For now, just know that everything's okay."

"It's not okay," Candy said, her face turning red with anger and defiance. "You…you…you *stole* me!"

The woman chuckled. "I like your feistiness, that's a very good sign, and yes, I suppose you could put it that way. I prefer to think of it more as rescuing you than stealing you, though. I thought I was saving you."

Candy screwed up her nose. The woman's gentle voice and easy, relaxed manner had gone some way to calming her. She'd listened to her talk with interest; the first real voice other than her father's that she'd heard for ages. She didn't know that it had been nearly two years. The words intrigued her. "Saving me from what? Was something really bad going to come and get me?"

"Oh, sweetheart, the really bad thing had already come for you, but I don't expect you to understand just yet. Give it all time, then we'll talk properly."

"But Daddy's not hurt?"

"No, he's absolutely fine."

Candy got the feeling that the lady wished that maybe wasn't the case. It didn't make her like her very much, but it did make her trust that she was telling the truth. If she didn't have to worry about Daddy, then all she had to worry about was herself. "Where am I and when will I be going home?"

"You're in the place where I live and we'll talk about you going home later, after you're over the shock. How do you feel? Are you still tired, would you like to go back to sleep for a little while longer?"

Candy shook her head, she felt like she'd slept longer than she had in ages. She was surprised when her hair felt swingy around her head and a fruity scent filled the air. She put her hand up to her head, puzzled by the soft, silky feel beneath her fingers.

The woman gave that small chuckle again, amused by her puzzlement. "The first thing we did was get you out of your pyjamas and give you a bath. It looked like you hadn't had one in a long time. Your hair is about three shades lighter now. Such a beautiful colour of blonde."

The woman raised her hand and gently stroked a strand of Candy's hair. For some reason, her touch reminded her of her mother. It made her feel less afraid. After all, if they were going to hurt her, they probably wouldn't have given her a bath and put her into this warm, cosy bed. She didn't know what was going on but she decided to wait and see. She spent most of her life waiting anyway so this was not much different and it was kind of nice to be around another person, especially one that was actually paying her some attention. It felt good. It also felt good to be clean. She couldn't remember the last time she'd had a proper bath. Normally, she washed herself with a flannel she wet under the cold water tap of the bath when her father was at work. He didn't seem to care much about her cleanliness and never commented on it. She only wished she could remember having the bath but funnily enough, she couldn't remember anything after she'd been carried out of her bedroom. She must have been too scared. That *was* something she was used to. When things were really, really bad, she found herself struggling to remember the details, as if her brain had just decided that she didn't need to know.

"If you're not sleepy anymore, would you like to get up and have some breakfast, are you hungry?"

Candy wasn't sure how to answer that. "I ate yesterday," she stammered, thinking it might be greedy to expect to do so again today.

The woman laughed again but it was tinged with a hint of sadness. "Kids are supposed to eat every day, Candy. In fact, they're supposed to eat at least three times a day and sometimes…" she leant in close and lowered her voice to a conspiratorial whisper. "…sometimes even with snacks or treats in between."

Candy studied her closely, sure she was lying to her or making fun of her, but her face was open and honest. Still, Candy wasn't sure. That cold, hard knot had gone from her tummy with her dinner last night and hadn't yet returned. She was used to not eating for days on end, either as punishment for being naughty or simply because her father forgot about her. Her tummy wasn't crying out for food so she saw no reason to eat.

"You really should try and have a little breakfast. It is the most important meal of the day you know."

Candy didn't know. For as long as she could clearly remember, meals were only dinner. She wasn't even sure what someone would eat in the morning. Somehow, the thin strips of meat in a watery gravy and synthetic tasting potatoes and carrots that came in those little sections of the plastic tray didn't appeal for during the daytime. Watching Candy's face and seeing all the emotions flooding across it, the woman made a decision.

"Right, let's get you dressed and then we'll go and see if I can tempt you with anything. Do you need to go to the bathroom first, it's right over there?"

Candy looked around the room she was in for the first time. It was quite a large room, painted a pale pastel pink. There was a large window covered by a matching shade of blind that was letting some sunlight shine through. A white door lay in the direction the lady had indicated and Candy assumed that was the bathroom. Right there, attached to her room? Did that mean it was her bathroom? She giggled at the thought. Whoever had heard of one person having a bathroom all to themselves? She grew a little more serious when she thought about how good it would be to have a door into the bathroom from her room for when Daddy locked her in at night. She was curious to see it but she didn't need to go right now so she thought would save that little bit of exciting exploration for later. For now, she carried on with her examination of the room.

As well as the bed she was in, there were two cabinets either side of it, the one closest to her holding a glass of water and an alarm clock. The clock made her giggle again. It had huge numbers and in the centre of them was a cheerful, smiling face. The hands of the clock were arms with big, gloved hands on the end, a finger pointing at the relevant numbers. Apart from the white face and gloves, it was brightly coloured in reds and yellows. It was such a happy looking thing that Candy could well imagine that waking up to see it would make her laugh every single day. She thought for a second that she absolutely had to learn to read the time so she could use it, but then she remembered that she wouldn't be here long enough.

With that thought comforting her as well as making her feel a little sad, she was curious to see what else might be in the room that would interest her. She drank it all in, seeing there was also a wardrobe and a dresser, and a low dressing table with a stool tucked neatly into the well. There was also a toy chest and a bookcase neatly filled with books. All the furniture was white but the stool was padded with a plush covering in a dusky pink, and the mirror sitting on top of the dressing table had gold trim. The deep pink, thick pile carpet matched the colouring of the stool cover perfectly. It was a beautiful room and she let her pleasure and excitement overwhelm her for a moment. It soon faded again as she remembered that she couldn't stay here. She had to go home.

"I don't need the bathroom," she said in a very small voice.

The woman tried to keep her own disappointment hidden from the little girl. She wasn't like any other child she'd ever come across before. Most would have been running all over this room by now, examining everything, laying claim to everything, trying it all out. She and her colleagues had put so much effort into it for her, hoping that Candy would be enchanted with her princess bedroom, but she didn't seem to have any point of reference for it and the enthusiasm that had crossed her face had been very short lived. She was so small and so young, yet somehow she seemed old, far older than she should ever be at her age. It was almost as if she didn't have any idea how to be a child, no idea how just to be carefree and happy. She decided it was her main mission to remedy that. If Candy agreed to stay, she would have some serious work ahead of her, but she needed to know how to be happy and how to play too. Play and fun were the key elements they used in their learning techniques. They were essential with the little ones. She never imagined she would ever face a situation where she would have to teach that first before they could start on the other things. Still, she was nothing if not up for a challenge.

"Okay then, let's go on over to the wardrobe and see what you want to wear today. I'm Jennifer by the way, but my friends call me Jen so that means you can too if you'd like?"

Candy nodded shyly and took the offered hand once she'd hopped out of bed. She revelled in the funny feel of the carpet between her toes as together they walked over to the wardrobe. Closer now, Candy could see that the white piece of furniture had gold stars dotted over the doors. They were so pretty she couldn't resist reaching out to touch one.

"Do you like them?" Jen asked. "I painted them for you because you're going to be our little rock star. I just know it."

Candy pulled open the wardrobe doors; once more, a frown marring her small face. "They aren't my clothes."

Jen realised she was going to have tread very carefully. Candy seemed desperate to need to hold onto the thought that she'd be going home soon, but their goal was to convince her otherwise. That was going to take time with this one.

"Oh well, we didn't really have time to pick up anything of your own, so these are yours while you're here."

"You mean I can borrow them, any of them?"

Jen thought of the hours she'd spent shopping choosing everything personally for the little girl that was soon to become her charge, handpicking everything that she'd have loved to have at her age but wasn't given the opportunity. She nodded and smiled. "Yes, you can borrow them."

There didn't seem any harm in going along with whatever she was comfortable with for now. She was rewarded by Candy finally showing some traits that Jen had expected from a little girl, delving into the wardrobe and examining the range of clothing with interest. There was everything she could possibly imagine, from casual sundresses to more elaborate fussy little gowns with frills and lace, to sparkly jeans and glittered t-shirts. There was also a range of footwear from sandals to trainers. Everything was in bright colours or pretty pastels. Many of the items adorned with patterns or characters, sparkly rhinestones, or more subtle glitter. It was an absolute treasure trove for a four-year-old girl and Jen watched with satisfaction as Candy was drawn to it all like a magpie. She smiled indulgently as Candy examined each piece with a mixture of excitement and interest, occasionally holding something up against her and checking out how it looked in the mirror on the inside of the child-height wardrobe door. She nodded in satisfaction. She'd triggered something in Candy, found something she could use, maybe even bargain with. It was a start.

Candy finally selected an outfit of a pair of dark blue jeans with glitter through the material and a shooting star made out of jewels on the back pocket, and a white t-shirt with bright red hearts on the front. She chose white trainers with a red stripe and laces to match. After being shown where to find underwear, she carried everything over to the bed and laid it all down carefully.

"Are you sure it's okay for me to borrow these?" Candy asked.

"Absolutely. Do you need help getting dressed?"

"No, I can do it."

Jen assumed that it was simply bravado on Candy's part and that eventually she'd get stuck and require her to step in. She didn't. She was actually incredibly accomplished and adept at dressing herself, even with tying the laces of her trainers. Jen didn't know whether to be delighted or to feel horrified that, obviously, her father hadn't even helped her dress in the mornings. She would be even more horrified if she'd known that apart from unlocking Candy's door, he never even saw or spoke to her in the mornings; he simply hurried downstairs to the kitchen and drank a quick cup of coffee while glancing over the morning paper before dashing out the door to work. She knew an awful lot about Candy's life but that was one fact that had escaped their research and careful surveillance. They could only see so much from their points of observation and Candy was so locked down it had been impossible to have any direct access to her. She was aware that there were blanks in their intel and filling them in was another major part of her aims here. She filed the information away and held out her hand to Candy.

"Come on, let's see about breakfast. I bet I'll find something you want to eat."

CHAPTER FOUR

"So, how are things progressing?"

Jen looked back to Candy, currently playing a lively game of tag in the gym hall with other kids of varying ages. Her face was flushed, her eyes had temporarily lost that dull, serious look and were sparkling, and she was laughing loudly. She turned back to Anthony, one of her closest colleagues. "I think it's going really well, all things considered."

"How long has she been here now?"

"Nine weeks, and I think it's a major breakthrough that she's been here this long. She spent the first three weeks constantly asking when she'd be going home. She still seems to have an absolutely unfailing loyalty to her father, even though he was a swine."

"Loyalty is a very good quality," Anthony uttered. "It bodes well for the future."

"Yes, I couldn't agree more, but the problem is that it's so misplaced. She had no idea how normal kids lived and, therefore, no idea that everything he was doing was actually child abuse. She'd never even seen the television other than the evening news. Her knowledge of current affairs was very impressive for her age, even if she didn't really understand the answers she was giving me. Anyway, convincing her of certain things was really hard, even down to the fact that three meals a day every day was normal, let alone being around other kids just to play."

"Maybe we should have waited until she'd started school. That way she would have learned how other kids live and what a normal life was like. That would have made this whole process so much easier."

"Maybe, but maybe not. Everything is so strange to her, everything is a surprise. She'll be much more open to hearing all about The Realm because of that. She'll take it as something else she never knew and that everyone else does. Plus, she's so starved of learning she soaks everything up like a sponge. She's so eager to be taught, she's a dream. She's very smart for her age so I'm going to have no problem with furthering her training, if only I can replace that loyalty to the scumbag. That's what this comes down to. Perhaps it might have been better if she'd had time to have a life outside her own four walls, but there was no way I could have left her there a minute longer. I had to get her away before he did some damage that would never heal."

"Talking of which, how is she now medically? I remember the first report and her malnutrition and dehydration were quite concerning, as were some of her injuries."

"Luckily for us, there weren't any serious breaks as I'm certain he wouldn't have dared take her to a hospital and they'd have been left to heal on their own, setting all wrong. There was evidence of an old fracture in her arm, but it was very small and healed perfectly. There was some very heavy and deep bruising, but they've all healed now and there was nothing else lasting. As for everything else, she is eating well now, putting on weight and grown a bit already too. Physically, she is going to be absolutely fine and is already just your average, normal little girl. Emotionally, she didn't really seem to have that many scars. She was miserable but couldn't really remember being any other way so she thought that was normal and because she didn't know she was living any differently from anyone else, wasn't as deeply traumatised as one would have expected. Due to lack of external stimulation, she does internalise a lot, though. Having nothing but her own thoughts to occupy her has made her rely solely on her own opinions and to overthink everything, but I'm sure I can assist her on how to use that as an advantage rather than a disadvantage. She is obviously still behind with learning as she never spent any time with an adult from whom she could pick things up, and didn't even see kids TV. I'm trying to catch her up on that, but her choice of viewing is still a bit young for her age. It's as if she needs to start from the very beginning, even though she could jump ahead if she wanted to.

"We've started on the basic reading too, but she's not so keen on book learning. She prefers listening." She glanced over at Candy again, smiling. "She absolutely loves physical exercise, though, which is great. Letting her into the gym hall was like letting a caged animal free in the wild for the first time. Now that she has a healthy diet and a small intake of the usual sugars and fats that kid have in their treat food, there is no stopping her and she never seems to get tired. In short, there's nothing there I can't work with if only I could broach the subject of her staying."

"Has she ever spoken of her mother?" Anthony asked.

Jen was quite for a moment before she answered, "Yes."

"And?"

"She doesn't know. Her father told her she left. Not only that but he seems to have made her believe it was her fault. The time she spoke of that was the only time I've seen her cry since the night I picked her up."

"Then use it."

Jen knew exactly what Anthony meant. The truth was that Candy's father had been lying to her—her mother was dead. She died in the line of duty, during a time when she had passed over control to someone else and should have already walked away from this life completely to concentrate on her own family. She was an amazing woman and she died a heroine. She left behind a life she loved for something she loved even more—her daughter. It was almost laughable to think that she would have walked away from her family because she didn't like her daughter, or at least it might have been if the lie wasn't so awful and had such a tragic effect on the little girl.

To tell Candy all this would expose her father for the liar he was, and Jen had no doubt that Candy would work out for herself that her father had done it deliberately to hurt her and make her feel bad because he couldn't cope with his own misery. Taking it out on her was his way of making his selfish-self feel better, and he did in the most despicable ways possible. Jen couldn't even begin to express the fury she'd felt when she realised that Candy blamed herself for driving her mother away. She contemplated Anthony's words and said, "It would be cruel, perhaps unnecessarily so."

"But it would be totally effective in breaking that misplaced loyalty," Anthony replied. "Especially with all the proof we have and could show her. Unless you think it will die away on its own over time and in time."

"I'm not so sure it will. She has a dream life here, but she still asks about him every single day and asks when she can see him. I really don't want her to ever see him again."

"Then do it."

Jen decided she would give it another couple of weeks and see what happened. She had to concede the point that it might be her only option to achieve what she herself wanted.

CHAPTER FIVE

"And kick, and kick, and again, and kick."

Jen held the pummel pads firmly as the eight-year-old Candy advanced and kicked, advanced and kicked in a volley of devastating sidekicks. Loud pop rock music flooded the gym and Candy was totally in the zone, the rhythm of her movement and breathing flawless.

The time that Jen had sat her down and told her all about her mother was only a distant memory to Candy. She knew everything now. She knew all about The Realm and the world of Gatekeepers, Seekers, and most significantly for her new role in life, Watchers. She knew about the history of the asteroid that had fragmented the world into thousands of pieces and left behind all those other strange worlds, and the gates that connected them to this world. She knew all about the dangers that lay behind those gates and the mission of The Realm always to keep them closed and the others who wanted to open them all, no matter what it would unleash upon this earth. She knew that she was in the Watcher Academy, training to be one herself one day. Most importantly, she knew all about her mother.

She'd learned that her mother had been a Watcher, a role that she'd embraced with all her heart, even after she'd fallen in love and gotten married. She hadn't wanted to give it up then, but when she became pregnant and was close to having a family of her own, she realised where her priories lay. Still, she'd wanted to handle the training of her replacement on her own, in spite of The Realm insisting that it could be taken care of by another. She'd insisted, finding it hard to trust anyone else with the care of her Gatekeeper. She'd been reluctant to let go completely even after the birth of her daughter and immersing herself into caring for her small family. She'd kept up visiting her Gatekeeper regularly. It had been terribly bad luck that two Seekers had attacked them when they were taking a walk in the park together and catching up. Seeing that the replacement Watcher was struggling to fight both of them and that her Gatekeeper was in mortal danger, she'd hadn't been able to stand idly by and hadn't even considered her own safety when she'd leapt into the fray to save her. Unfortunately, although she saved the lives of her Gatekeeper and her Watcher, she wasn't so lucky and sustained an injury that turned out to be fatal a few hours later.

While Candy had no problem processing the information about the gates and the strange things that were kept hidden from the majority of the world, she'd taken a long time to process her thoughts on hearing the truth about her mother. She'd been hit by a wave of sadness for this woman who'd given birth to her but whom she hardly knew. She hadn't seriously expected to see her ever again but the cold hard fact that it would never be possible meant she experienced the grief of her loss just the same. At her tender age, she also couldn't help the self-pity that came along with those feelings. She cried a lot. She was ashamed to say that she also felt some anger towards her. If she'd put her own family first before her love and loyalty towards her watcher then she'd still be alive. There was no real need for her to be where she was on the day she'd died. She could have still been here for them, then her Daddy wouldn't have hated her, and her life could have been very different. She understood by then that her childhood hadn't been normal, not by a long shot.

She didn't even know what to think about her father. On one hand, she understood why he was so angry all the time now. She felt angry at her mother, too, so she thought that it was okay for him to feel that way. Maybe he felt guilty as well. Candy didn't know much about the world but it was her perception then that the daddy was the one that should take care of the family. Maybe he thought it was somehow his fault or he'd done something wrong and it was eating him up inside like things did when she'd wet herself or had to steal something to eat. She could understand that.

On the other hand, he'd lied to her. Not only had he told her that her mother had left them by choice, he'd told her it was her fault. She'd blamed herself all this time for both their suffering. He'd made her believe that she was such a bad girl she'd driven her mother away, as her mother just couldn't stand her for another minute. Even Candy understood that this was a horrible thing to do to another human being. She couldn't help but be furious with him for how bad he'd made her feel or that he'd deliberately not told the truth. It shattered apart everything she thought she knew about her relationship with her daddy. She couldn't not feel sad about that either. Maybe if he hadn't lied and talked about Mummy it would have helped him, maybe *she* could have helped him.

These horrible mixes of conflicting emotions were almost too much for her to handle. She'd shut herself away in her room as she'd tried to work it all out, finding solace in all the pretty things there, spending hours playing dress up with the extensive wardrobe and all the pretty jewellery and hair clips in her dressing table. She found comfort in them, something to keep her occupied and distracted on the surface while the deeper parts of her mind managed to address these huge issues without them overwhelming her. She'd delved into the toy chest and used the dolls there first to act out real scenarios from her life as well as the imaginary ones that could have been if her life had been different. It helped work it all out in her young mind. In many ways, this time very much shaped Candy into the person she would become. There was one thing that wasn't in any doubt, though, the revelations had exactly the effect that those that ran the Watcher academy had hoped for—the loyalty to her father and desire to go home was gone forever.

When Candy had finally emerged from her room, she was ready to face the world and embrace her new life as a Watcher.

Much to Jen and the others' delight, Candy flung herself wholeheartedly into everything the academy had to offer and found herself rewarded for her efforts in abundance. She felt that no matter how much she gave, they returned it tenfold. For the first time, she found herself loved, wanted, and maybe even needed. She liked being warm, safe, and well fed. She liked not having achy bits and tender bruises. She liked having company whenever she wanted it and solitude when she sought it, but most of all, she liked this feeling of being embraced by what she now thought of as her new real family. This was a completely different life and she loved it.

Slowly, she learned much more about what a normal childhood should have been, and she also learned that many of the children in the academy with her hadn't had that type of normal life either. Some of them had similar stories of neglect and abuse, some of them didn't have mummies and daddies at all, and others had happy childhoods but had been raised knowing all about their Watcher parents and had come to the academy voluntarily when they were of age. These were the lucky ones, who not only had the academy family, but also had visits arranged every week with their loving, smiling parents, so proud of the family line being carried on and their children following in their footsteps. Candy didn't even feel jealous or remorseful that she didn't and could never have that, she had everything she could possibly want here as it was. She was determined that she would survive, thrive, and repay the kindness of Jen and the others by being the best Watcher they'd ever had.

She'd thrown herself into her Watcher, learning, but most of all, she'd embraced the physical training. That was the part Candy liked the best. They'd called it gym class at first, playing lots of different types of games with different instructors, none of the little tots realising that they were being introduced to the basic training for several disciplines of martial arts amongst various other styles of fighting in which they would all eventually become experts. When Candy finally realised this she loved it even more, she loved feeling tough. She was determined to learn and practice as much as possible. No slimy Seeker was ever going to do to her what they'd done to her mother or ever get their hands on her Gatekeeper when she eventually had one. She'd kick their backsides from kingdom come and back again if they so much as tried.

And so Candy continued to live and train at the academy. Jen could never inspire a love of academic learning in her in the way she had on everything from how to be a girl to how to take down an opponent, but she got her to a level where she could scrape through some exams. It wasn't that she wasn't smart enough, only that she simply wasn't interested and wouldn't apply herself. As far as Candy was concerned, she would never need it and had far more important things to do with her life. Jen didn't agree but there was little she could do.

After she'd sat her exams and she'd expressed no desire to continue her home schooling to any further level, Jen had sat down and spoken to her about her future, saying that she needed to start finding her way out in the real world. Candy decided that she would study a beauty course at the local college and before she knew it, her graduation and her eighteenth birthday were just around the corner. She was pretty sure she knew what was coming when Jen came to her room for a private conversation. She bet she was going to offer to have a celebration of some sort.

"Well, Candy, I hear congratulations are in order for you passing your course with flying colours," Jen said, smiling.

"Yeah! How cool is that? I graduate next week and once I have my certificates I'll be able to try and get a job in a salon or a spa or something. I want to take you out to lunch or even dinner, maybe with my very first wages, as a kind of a thank you."

"That's nice of you, I'd like that very much," Jen said with a smile. "But you might change your mind after you've heard what I have to say."

Candy's excitement faded and her face fell. "Oh."

Jen struggled to keep the sympathy and sadness from showing on her own face and cleared her throat so that she could prevent her voice from breaking. "You'll be eighteen in a few weeks. I'm afraid our rules mean that you can't stay here anymore. You'll have to find your own place in life. Of course, The Realm and all of us will always be here for you as advisors, friends, and family, but in order to be the best you can be, you have to stand on your own two feet, out in the world alone."

Candy's bottom lip trembled. "I have to leave?"

"Yes, it's time, Candy."

Candy crawled over from the side of her bed to the centre to lean her back against her headboard, tucking her knees up to her chin and holding them tight as she'd used to do to comfort herself as a small child. She resisted the urge to rock back and forth as she digested this unwelcome information.

"It's not that bad," Jen reassured her. "I'm sure you'll take to having your own place and your independence just as well as you took to coming here. Besides, I haven't told you everything yet."

"I don't know if I want to hear anymore right now," Candy muttered.

"I think you'll like everything else I have to say a lot better. Once you find yourself a job, we'll help you find a really nice flat or something that you can afford. We'll pay the rent for the first three months until you find your feet and work out your budget plan. We'll even help with the decorating and furnishing. I could shop with you, if you'd like?"

Jen tried not to sound too hopeful as she stared anxiously at Candy. She would very much like to remain her friend and be part of her life beyond being her main mentor and trainer. It didn't often happen and sometimes it wasn't the best idea. Jen had no doubt that once Candy found her own way, she'd have no more need of her and would soon forget about her, but she hoped she could hold onto their closeness for a little longer. Candy had been so little and so lost when she'd taken her, and she felt she'd raised her. She was like an actual daughter to her.

Candy was still in a turmoil over the news, but she'd grown up enough to know that there were rules Jen had to follow. This wasn't her fault and there was no point in sulking with her over it and ruining the last of their time together. "I'd like that. It would be fun."

Jen beamed. "Terrific. We'll have a great time making some little place your very own, and it'll soon feel more like home than anywhere you've ever lived before. And I haven't even told you the very best bit yet. As soon as we think you're settled enough, we'll be assigning you to your mission."

This caught Candy's attention. Abandoning her self-comforting position, she practically flung herself back to sit on the edge of the bed next to Jen, her eyes shining with excitement. "Mission? You mean like a real Watcher assignment?"

"Yes, Candy. Not only is it time for you to take your place in life, it's also time for you to take your place as a Watcher. You're going to be allocated to a possible Gatekeeper."

Chapter Six

Candy tossed her jacket and bag onto the couch after she let herself into her little flat after a day's work, not even thinking about the fact that her dad used to do the exact same thing with his jacket every day too. For the most part, he was nothing but a vague, distant memory.

She took a moment to look around the room and sighed in satisfaction. Jen had been right; she'd taken to having her own place like a duck to water. She'd loved making it her own and had refused financial help from The Realm, insisting she paid for all her decorating materials and new furnishings herself out of her wages. It had felt terrific and now she could stand here and know that everything around her had been earned by her own hard work. Learning to budget money had been tough, but she'd insisted on learning the hard way in that too, having to make do with very little until the next payday if she went a little too wild in the DIY or furniture store. She'd learned to slow down and do things step by step when she could afford it. It made every task she completed and every item she acquired all the more special.

She headed through to her galley kitchen to see what she could make for dinner. The one thing she couldn't handle and swore she would never even so much as look at again was ready packaged, frozen, microwave meals. Also, as a beautician, she knew very well the wonders a good, healthy diet could do for a girl's skin, hair, and nails, not to mention her figure. As she peeled and chopped the vegetables, she contemplated whether she'd made any progress today or if in fact, she'd done the very opposite.

Although she'd had to apply and get her current job on her own merit, The Realm had pointed her in the right direction of a particular salon where working would also further her other goal—finding a way to insert herself into her possible Gatekeeper's life. She remembered the conversation with Jen very well. She thought it over again now as she carried out her meal preparation.

"Candy, you know your mother was a great Watcher, one of the best that this academy has ever produced? Well, we've all been watching you very closely as you've progressed over the years and The Realm feel that you could well be on your way to reaching those same heights. We think with a bit of experience and maturity you're going to be amazing. As such, The Realm is considering assigning you to what might be a very special Gatekeeper. Do you think you'd be up to the task?"

Candy knew this was a serious question. All Gatekeepers were incredibly special, so if this one was considered more special than most it would not only be a great honour to be assigned to him, but also a massive responsibility. She knew she needed to be certain within herself that she could handle it. A strong Gatekeeper would attract more attention and therefore more Seekers. It would be a hard task to keep them safe and her life would frequently be in danger. She had to be honest, not only with Jill, but also with herself. She gave herself time to think about it but finally, she nodded. "Yes, I'm ready. I accept all the implications that it would bring and I'm sure I can handle it as well as anyone else."

"Good girl. Obviously, you'll receive a complete dossier and until you've read that in detail, we won't expect a final decision. In the meantime, would you like to hear a little about him?"

"Yes, please."

Jen had gone on to explain that David's grandfather was on The Realm's list of exceptional people, one of their most special and powerful Gatekeepers whose abilities surpassed the others. He had that special something that just wasn't quantifiable. They had expected his daughter to carry on the line and when she hadn't, they were convinced that his grandson, David, would be the next Gatekeeper in the family. They had very high hopes for him too and as such, wanted to assign a Watcher earlier than normal, before anyone was sure if he was even going to be a Gatekeeper or not. This was unusual but not completely unheard of in the history books. Candy had been very intrigued and wanted to hear more.

"He's a very shy boy, very bookish and studious, and not at all sporty," Jen commented.

Candy laughed. "You mean he's a nerd? Oh, Lord, can you imagine me and a bookworm getting along?"

Jen laughed along with her but disagreed with her. "Actually, it's one of the reasons why we think you'd be a great pairing. You'll complement one another, both having very different areas of expertise and knowledge."

"Like two halves of a whole?" Candy asked thoughtfully.

"Yes, something like that."

"Yeah, okay, I can see how that would maybe work, but I can't see how I would get to know him in the first place, to find a place in his life where I could be close to him. We'll be so different that it would be really hard. Even if I pretended to like books and stuff, I'm sure he'd find me out the minute I tried to talk in depth about anything I was pretending to like or know about."

"Hmmm," Jen said, giving Candy a sly look. "If only you'd thought that anything you learned from a book could actually come in useful later in your life and actually studied. That would have been handy now wouldn't it?"

Candy had laughed again, known she'd been well and truly chastised and teased at the same time. "Can't argue with that and it's my bad, but that means I have to figure out another way."

"Actually, The Realm might have come up with something for you. There's a beauty salon in his city that's hiring right now. It just happens to be the one his mother goes to twice a week."

"Right," Candy said, catching on. "Make friends with the mother rather than the son… Sure, that could work. What do I do?"

"You're pretty much on your own from here on. I'll give you the salon details, then you'll have to apply for the job and do your best to get it. From there on, it'll be up to you to make sure you find a way into his life. If you don't get the job, you'll have to come up with something else. You have some time. David is a few months away from being twelve, so you've got just over a year to make sure you're there and keeping a close eye on him when he reaches his thirteenth birthday. So what do you think, interested enough for me to bring you all the files?"

"Absolutely," Candy said with a grin, excited at the idea of embarking upon her covert mission and being trusted with so much responsibility.

That was how Candy first heard of David Edwards. After reading his entire file, she felt even prouder that she'd been chosen to be his Watcher should he need one and still felt that way today. She'd managed to get the job at the salon and made sure she soon had David's mother, Jill, as one of her clients. From there, she'd managed to develop the usual rapport with her, beginning with the normal small talk about weather and holidays, then progressing to sharing small details of their lives, and Jill occasionally mentioning her son and superficial details of his life, too. Chatting easily and laughing a lot, they were certainly acquaintances that were friendly, but Candy wouldn't have gone so far as to say they were friends yet.

Today, she'd tried to take another step forward in that area. Casually, she'd introduced a new juice bar that had opened up not far from the salon and had spent the next fifteen minutes explaining the benefits of various juice mixtures as she'd given Jill her usual weekly manicure and pedicure. Then, before Candy ran out of things to say about juicing, she casually slipped into the conversation that maybe they could go there together so she could point her in the right direction of what would benefit Jill's skin the most from the menu selection.

Jill had seemed a little surprised by the suggestion, taken aback even. She'd said that she would have to check her diary and see if there was a day when she was free and let her know the next time she came in. She'd left in more of a hurry than usual. Now Candy was concerned. Maybe she'd moved too fast, pushed too hard. If she'd blown her best shot of finding a way into the Gatekeeper's life, then she'll never forgive herself. She tried to comfort herself with the fact that Jill hadn't actually given her an outright refusal. That had to be a good sign, right? Of course, there was also the very worst-case scenario that hadn't occurred to her before but certainly came to her now. What if she'd really crossed some boundary and Jill complained to her boss? What if she lost her job and therefore all contact with Jill? She felt like kicking herself. She should have been more subtle, maybe waiting until Jill revealed something in casual conversation that would have allowed Candy to bump into her accidentally on purpose. That would have been so much better.

"I'm an idiot," she muttered to herself, throwing down the carrot and the peeler she was holding.

Suddenly, she'd lost her appetite.

~*~

Two weeks had passed and the good thing was that Candy's boss hadn't pulled her aside and told her she was fired or even so much as given her a verbal warning. The bad thing was that Jill hadn't been back to the salon.

It was Friday and Candy was miserable as she entered the salon that morning. She just knew she'd scared Jill off and now it would be even harder to find another way in. If she turned up in Jill's life in another capacity, she would look like some creepy stalker and Jill would probably take out a restraining order against her or something. Quieter than usual, she hung up her jacket and went over to prepare her nail station for the day. She was always at the nail bar on Tuesdays and Fridays, doing other beauty treatments on the other days of the week. Once seated, she scanned through the list of appointments for the day that the receptionist had placed on her station for her, hoping to see Jill's name there. There was no sign of it. She sighed with disappointment.

Ten minutes before her lunch break, her day turned around completely.

Candy was busy tidying, having finished up with her last client for the morning a little early. The door burst open and a harried woman dressed in a bright skirt and floral-patterned top rushed in and made a beeline for Candy.

It was Jill.

"Hi, gosh, I'm sorry I haven't been in recently. It's been one of those times. First, my mother had a fall and was in hospital for a couple of days and needed my help to look after her once she came home, then my car broke down, and…well…it doesn't matter, it's just been one of those times and finding a spare moment for my facials and manicures was just impossible. Anyway, my nails are in a terrible state and I have a dinner date tonight. The pedicure isn't important, but I'd really like the manicure. I don't suppose there's any chance you could fit me in today, is there? It's an emergency!"

Candy grinned at Jill, flooded with relief and happiness at the same time. "Let me see what I can do. You are a VIP client after all."

Checking her book, she found she was fully booked for the afternoon. She frowned and chewed at her bottom lip. Jill saw her expression and guessed the problem. "You don't have a slot free, do you? That's okay. It doesn't matter. Thanks for looking anyway."

"Why don't I check and see if any of the others can fit you in?"

Jill shook her head. "That's okay. I was hoping for something really special, something truly outstanding and eye-catching. No one else does that like you can."

Suddenly, the perfect solution dawned on Candy. "Oh, duh! I'm so dumb sometimes. I was just about to go for lunch, but I wasn't planning on doing anything much anyway. If you've got the time, why don't we just do it right now?"

Jill looked pleased and surprised. "You'd give up your lunch break for me?"

"Of course. We can't have you going on a date night without spectacular nails. Take a seat. Now, we've only got an hour, so we'll be limited, but here's what I'm thinking…"

Ten minutes before her lunch hour was up, Candy was sitting back and admiring her handiwork, feeling pleased with the beautiful design she'd accomplished in such a short time that suited Jill's flamboyant tastes and sunny personality perfectly. "What do you think?" she asked with some anxiousness that maybe Jill wouldn't be as pleased with her work as she was.

"They're perfect! They're going to look fabulous with that outfit I described to you. You've got such a natural talent for this. I love them."

Candy beamed with pleasure.

"I don't suppose you could do me a massive favour, could you? I don't want to smudge my wet nails, so could you pop your hand into my handbag, grab my phone and text someone for me? My car is still in the garage so I need to be picked up. It'll likely take them the length of time my nails take to dry to get here."

"Oh, no problem. Pop your hands in here and then I'll come round and get your phone."

With Jill sitting with her hands in the nail drier, she instructed Candy on who to text and what to say.

Candy had just seen her over to the reception desk so she could settle up at the till when the door opened. Expecting her next customer, Candy looked up with a welcoming smile on her face.

Much to her surprise, it wasn't her regular client but an older man dressed in a very smart suit and a nice shirt and tie. She was instantly attracted to him, thinking he was very handsome and had the kindest, most gentle eyes that she'd ever seen before in her life. Their eyes met and he returned her smile. She felt a little flutter of butterflies. He really had a very nice smile; warm, reassuring somehow.

Jill glanced around to see whom Candy was smiling at. She broke into a smile herself. "Oh, there you are, William. Thanks so much for doing this for me. My car will be ready soon, I promise."

"It's no problem at all," William said as he sauntered over to them, trying to look at Jill but unable to keep his eyes straying back to Candy.

Candy felt herself blushing. She'd always attracted a lot of attention from the boys in the academy but had never been able to think of them as anything other than brothers. They were family to her so trying to think of them any other way was just gross. She was not short of male admirers once she'd left the academy either, but once again, she wasn't interested. She knew she wasn't that clever and not that mature, but the boys her own age just didn't appeal to her. Most times, they were focused on having fun. She had much bigger things to think about in life, a greater purpose. She didn't have time to spend on just having fun. She didn't want to admit to herself that she was at all damaged by her abusive father or that it affected the way she interacted with boys, so that was something she buried very deep and refused to ever think about, making other excuses about why she wasn't interested in anyone who asked her out or showed any interest in her. In contradiction to everything above, she definitely felt an interest in this man that she'd never felt before. She felt drawn to him. She looked toward Jill, hoping for an introduction.

Jill obliged. "This is my beautician, Candy. Candy, this is my husband, William."

Candy couldn't understand why it felt as if her heart had dropped into her pink leather, studded, high-heeled boots, but the disappointment she felt that he was taken was crushing. The brightness in her smile faded and when she held out a hand to shake the one offered to her, it was limp and half-hearted. In contrast, his was firm and lingered, perhaps a moment too long. Candy really hoped that Jill hadn't noticed anything untoward about the way she'd looked at her husband. Luckily, she didn't seem to.

"Thanks so much for doing this, Candy," Jill said. "You're an absolute lifesaver. I'll make sure I give you an even more glowing recommendation to all my friends when they ask who did my nails, not that I don't already, though." Jill accompanied her words with a very generous tip. "I'd best not keep William waiting since he's been good enough to interrupt his day to collect me. Oh, and about trying out that juice bar together, how about we go on Sunday when the salon's closed and you're off? I could make it around eleven if that's suitable?"

"Oh, yeah, yeah, that'd be great."

"Come on, love, I've got to get back to work," William said, placing a casual arm around Jill's shoulders.

He steered her in the direction of the door and holding it open for Jill to exit, he looked back to where Candy stood deflated at the counter. "It was nice to meet you. I hope it happens again sometime, and just so you know, it's ex-husband. She forgets that part sometimes."

Candy's heart soared as he gave that warm smile again before disappearing out of the door and letting it close behind him. Suddenly, everything in her world looked a whole lot brighter.

CHAPTER SEVEN

"May I ask you about something?"

Candy was sitting in a coffee shop with Jen, having one of their regular meetings to catch up and to report in. A public place hadn't seemed the smartest choice to her at first, but once Jen had explained that she couldn't ever come back to the academy now that she was out in the world in case she was followed, and that she couldn't be seen coming and going from Candy's apartment too often in case someone knew who she was and figured out Candy was a Watcher, she'd seen that it was the sensible option after all. They always picked one of the most popular ones at the busiest times so that it was crowded and noisy. Provided they waited to grab a table for two so no one could join them, they could talk with hardly any chance of being overheard, and even if someone was spying from a short distance away with one of those listening devices, they wouldn't be able to hone in on their specific conversation over the racket of chatter, called orders, and the incredibly noisy coffee machines.

She regarded Jen with a grin, wondering which particular aspect of her life she wanted more information on as she had so much to choose from. It had gone through some dramatic changes over the last seven or eight months.

"Sure, go ahead," Candy replied.

"Please don't take offence at the question, but are you certain you're just not with this man because of his son? I know we asked you to find a way into your possible charge's life, but that would be taking it too far for any Watcher, even for The Realm themselves. I know thcy usually say any means possible, but they would frown upon using a relationship that involved in that way."

Candy shook her head. "No offence taken. I can see why it would look that way, I mean, it totally does. I get it. That's not what happened, though. I was making good progress with Jill; I really was on track with that but in the process, I got to know William, too."

"That's her ex-husband?"

"Yeah, and I really, really liked him. He made me feel safe somehow, and interestingly, he makes me feel like I'm the most special person in the whole wide world, like the sun and moon to him, you know?"

"As if his world would collapse without you?"

"Exactly! I know it seems like a huge coincidence but it really is how it happened. I'd see him along with

Jill sometimes and we got more and more interested, and so we started seeing one another without Jill, and then we fell in love. I think I fell in love the very first time I saw him," she added with an embarrassed blush and giggle.

Jen smiled, not mentioning that she thought she knew exactly why William Edwards had been the one to capture Candy's heart. He was so much older than Candy, but she'd done her research. He was a gentle, kind, patient man, who didn't have a temper or a mean bone in his body. The way he cared for Candy was more than likely providing her with the father figure she should have had and probably longed for, even if she didn't realise it.

"As long as you're both happy, then I'm very pleased for you. What about Jill, how does she feel about all this?"

"I don't think she's all that happy about it," Candy said, her face turning sad. "She definitely wasn't to start with, then she seemed to accept it, but I think she thought it was just a fleeting infatuation and would fade out. She's definitely not happy about me moving in and had a lot to say about me giving up my job immediately afterwards. I guess it looked like I was a gold digger or a bimbo that had been looking for a sugar daddy to keep her."

"Oh yes, that's right, William still lives with Jill and David. That's a very strange set up."

"I know, right? Well, it means David has both his parents around and that's what matters. I'm not going to complain because that's three of us keeping an eye on him and keeping him safe."

"And how is your relationship with him?"

"I don't think he likes me much either. I do keep trying with him, but he always just seems to be really uncomfortable with me. He doesn't talk much and usually tries to be wherever I'm not. I feel pretty rejected if I'm honest."

"Don't worry about it. This is quite normal and it's probably so strained because you're his father's girlfriend."

"Oh, I hadn't thought about that!" Candy said. "Is it a mistake? Do you think it's interfering with my job? Do you think I should give up William for David?"

Jen reached over and placed a hand on Candy's. "Let's give it a little while and see what happens. I'm sure it'll work itself out eventually. The sugar daddy thing will go away over time once Jill sees that you're genuinely in love. And as for David, well, it often takes a while for the Gatekeeper to accept a Watcher in his life, especially as it's so intense and full on. Try to always be there but keep as low a profile as possible. Try not to let him know you're watching him all the time."

"I'll do my best. I think I'm doing okay. He definitely doesn't know I watch him at school, or when he's out with his little friend. There haven't been any signs of anything yet, nothing to let me know if he's going to be a Gatekeeper or not. What happens if he isn't?"

"There not being any signs of anything yet with David is to be expected. We've got another week before his thirteenth birthday and nothing will happen before then so don't panic about that. But to answer your question, if it turns out that he isn't a Gatekeeper, then you'd have to be assigned to another."

"So that would mean I would have to leave William?"

"Either that or give up being a Watcher. You know you have to be around or at least nearby the Gatekeeper almost all the time. I don't think you'll have to worry about that, though. I'm certain that this line won't skip more than one generation. Everything will work out."

"You really think so?"

"Yes, I really do."

Candy was happy again. If Jen told her everything would work out, then she should stop worrying about it and just let it happen. In the meantime, she would be right there for David the minute something happened.

~*~

It turned out that it happened earlier than she expected, and she wasn't really prepared for it. The day before David's birthday, he started acting very oddly indeed.

His birthday party, such as it was, was happening a day early simply so that the whole family could make it. Candy didn't think it was much of a party. He was going to be a teenager and she knew exactly what sort of party she'd organise for an event like that. It would be a mixed boy/girl party with cool decorations and a rocking DJ. There would be massive speakers, low lighting, an illuminated dance floor, and music pumping to the point you had to yell to talk over it, and the occasional slow number for a chance to dance closer together. The food would be finger food but not a naff, old-fashioned buffet with a few sad-looking scotch eggs and tired old vol-au-vents filled with stuff you couldn't even tell what it was meant to be, but exciting platters with tasty stuff you could be romantic sharing. That was the type of party a teenager should have. No one else in the household agreed with her, though, not even David. He didn't even want a party at all. He was such a strange kid.

She didn't know if she'll ever understand him. Sometimes it made her despair that they would ever have the type of relationship she'd imagined she would have with her Gatekeeper. On hearing about how close her mum was to her's, she'd expected that too and had thought it might have come easily, as if somehow they would recognise one another without it ever having to be spoken about. No such luck. He was still doing his best to avoid her at all costs. The way things were between them made her wonder how it would ever work when she was his step mum as well as his Watcher, but she told herself to put those thoughts right out of her head. William hadn't asked her to marry him and just because she wanted him to didn't mean to say he ever would. Besides, she had enough problems without thinking about the ones that might never happen.

She'd been having all these thoughts while she was in the bathroom applying her makeup. That was when she heard David scream.

She responded in a flash, dropping everything, and dashing out of the bathroom she shared with William with only one eye done, not caring that she would look totally stupid.

She got out into the hallway just in time to see David flying downstairs as if he were running for his very life. She dashed into his bedroom, doing a quick check for intruders first but on finding nothing untoward in there, as silent as a cat, she streaked downstairs after him.

She came to a sudden stop as she heard voices in the hallway. She heard Jill ask David what the matter was and she listened intently to his response. Something was out in the garden! She hurried down the last few steps and was about to dash into the kitchen when Jill's words stopped her again.

"I can't see anything at all. What is it I'm looking for and where was it?"

Candy waited with baited breath to hear David's answer.

"I don't know what it was. It wasn't like anything I've seen before or even read about. It was on my swing."

The tremble in his voice portrayed his utter terror. Candy knew that David was timid and shy, but he was also logical and practical. He wasn't the type of kid to think there were monsters under his bed or hiding in his wardrobe. If he'd seen something, then something had definitely been there. She nodded sagely to herself while also experiencing a thrill of excitement and happiness. It was early, but it was happening, she was sure of it!

Listening to Jill confirm there was nothing there now and David failing to back up his claim or describe what he'd seen, she was left in no doubt. David was a Gatekeeper. She had her very own charge now and she would get to stay here. Life couldn't be any better, except for poor David of course. She knew that he might struggle more than most. He wasn't confident, wasn't sporty, wasn't confrontational or outgoing, and his rational mind would fight against anything beyond the accepted normal human realms. Coming to terms with the whole other Realm thing would mess with his head big time.

She decided there wasn't much she could do for him right now. She'd learned in her training that what the Gatekeepers usually encountered first was the Hoogle, and that they were pesky things but not normally life threatening. They would do everything in their power to confuse you, to slow you down, to frighten you even, but they didn't usually hurt anyone. Also, whatever it had been was outside so he wasn't in any immediate danger even if it wasn't a Hoogle.

David needed time to figure this out and since he'd faltered in even talking to his mum, the last thing he would want was her knowing what had just happened. It would only make him want to distance himself from her even more than he was already, and there was no way he was ready to hear about what she was to be to him for as long as he or she lived. That would totally freak him out. No, Jen had said that things would work themselves out over time so that's what she had to give it—time. Her best bet right now would be to go back upstairs and finish getting ready before someone saw her out here eavesdropping. It was better all-round if no one knew she'd seen or heard anything. Besides, she would literally die on the spot of embarrassment if anyone saw her with only half her face done. She must look *ridiculous.* She would keep the bedroom and bathroom door open so she could listen out for anything else happening and get back down as quickly as possible, pretending she was coming down for the first time that day.

She practically skipped back up the stairs. Everything was coming together exactly as it should be. She could stay with the man she loved and be around her Gatekeeper, taking it slow and letting him and their relationship develop. With The Realm believing they were both going to be a little bit special, they were going to make an amazing team one day; Candy couldn't wait.

CHAPTER EIGHT

Candy was looking forward to the family dinner. She had to admit she'd enjoyed David's party more than she thought she would. She was so happy at the turn of events and so excited about everything to come that she'd been giddy all day and thrown herself wholeheartedly into the celebration, probably more than David had. She'd made a real effort to engage him both yesterday and today. His rejection had stung a little but she held on to Jen's words like a mantra and they got her through.

As usual, she'd had to find an excuse to beg off the after breakfast chores this morning so she could disappear and follow David. Ugh, what was it with him and Billie, David's friend, that they liked hanging out in the woods so much? She'd been freezing as she stood guard at the base of the treehouse. Mind you, overhearing snippets of their conversation had given her some insights into their friendship that she would have to mull over. Maybe she could take a few lessons from Billie on how to be what David wanted and needed from his friends so that she might become one of them one day. Of course, her idea for the dinner for tonight had been shot down in flames by almost everyone but that was okay. She hated fast food anyway, so unhealthy, but she'd thought David might like it but his afraid to ask for it. Turns out that wasn't the case. Never mind. It would be easier to keep an eye on David at home anyway. Although things had started to happen yesterday, she was sure something else would happen on his actual birthday, maybe even something a lot bigger. She'd be keeping a much closer eye on him from on, and now that it was looking like it might be official, she'd be ready for anything. With that in mind, she slipped her feet into a pair of ballet flats instead of her usual heels and headed downstairs to join the others around the table.

It turned out to be quite a quiet affair. David was his usual withdrawn self and Jill's second husband, Andrew, seemed to be in a sulk over something. For once, she managed to resist the urge to cover the tension and awkward silences with a happy chatter. Instead, she watched and thought.

She wasn't quite sure what she made of Andrew. Sure, she was glad that Jill had fallen in love and married again because that meant William was free and Jill couldn't really complain that he had another relationship of his own. It made everything equal and that was a huge plus. On the other hand, there was something about Andrew that she didn't quite like. It was none of her business really. Sharing a house with him was more than worth it to be this close to David and to be with William, and if Jill was happy, then that's all that mattered, but he made Candy feel uneasy. It wasn't like he'd ever said anything inappropriate or mean or even so much as looked at her the wrong way, and he did seem to really love David and make every effort to be a friend and father to him, but still… She wished she had the words to describe it as that might help make it clearer in her head but she didn't, nor did she have any reason to feel the way she did. She didn't have anyone she could talk that over with either. The relationship between William and Andrew could be strained as it was, so she wasn't going to say anything that could make it worse. She knew this was a bit of a weird set up and that the dynamics were carefully balanced. The slightest thing could throw them out of whack and jeopardise the whole situation. If the family decided to move into separate houses, then David would stay with his mother. That would make everything much harder so she kept her thoughts on Andrew to herself and decided just to keep a close eye on him.

That was where her mind was – although to any onlooker, it would likely look like she was examining and dissecting her desert, probably trying to work out how many calories were in it – when from the corner of her eye, she saw David freeze and an expression of horror spread across his face. He was seeing something! Muscles tensed, she was ready to act if he was in danger, even if it meant revealing herself for what she was. She almost leapt to her feet when he screamed and leapt away from the table. *Wait,* she told herself, *it might be a Hoogle. Don't give the game away if you don't have to. You don't know what anyone else knows. Just hang on a little longer.*

She knew exactly what was happening when she saw the realisation dawn on David's face that no one else could see what he was seeing. She had a good idea what that would be doing to his head, messing with it big time, almost as much as what he was seeing would be. He would think he was going nuts. By the way, his eyes were almost popping out of their sockets and his head was whipping back and forth, he was seeing more than one thing. It looked as if he was surrounded by them. Nothing was attacking him, though; she'd know if it was and then she'd be there in a heartbeat, so she shouldn't do anything more in front of the norms just yet. She knew how important it was to keep the secrets from them. She watched carefully as David backed up further away from them, then finally turned and fled from the room. She heard his footsteps pound up the stairs and the bathroom door slam.

"Well, what the devil was that all about?!" William exclaimed, both incredulous and concerned. "I should go and talk to him."

Candy desperately wanted to offer to go, to be the one to comfort and console him and explain that he wasn't going crazy, to tell him the fascinating stories of the gates and The Realm, and the really important role he was to play. But she knew it would be pointless as he thought she was an imbecile. He wouldn't believe her, nor would he thank her for trying to help him. She felt sad as she watched Jill shake her head at William.

"It's okay. You stay here. I should be the one that goes." She smiled at Andrew apologetically.

"Probably just teenage hormones. Sorry everyone that the nice dinner was ruined."

Andrew reached out and squeezed her hand. "It wasn't. It was a lovely meal and it was almost over anyway. I could go if you want, you know, do the man to man thing?"

Jill patted the hand that was holding hers. "Thanks, love, but I'll go on up and see to him. I can always call either of you if I think it's something one of you would handle better, but I need to see for myself that he's okay first."

Both Andrew and William accepted her decision, preventing any conflict between them. Candy considered inventing a reason to excuse herself from the table so she could go and listen to what was being said and to check on David herself but as Jill had said, she would call them if David needed them. She also knew from the files she'd read that it was Jill who carried the line. She was the one that had grown up in a family connected with The Realm. She could probably imagine the conversation that would be going on upstairs between the two. For now, she needed to give them complete privacy.

CHAPTER NINE

Candy had been trying really hard with David. Ever since his thirteenth birthday, she was absolutely certain Jill must have had the talk with him, and not the one about the birds and the bees. He must know all about the other worlds, The Realm, and the fact that he was a Gatekeeper. She was hoping that along with that information would come some clarity, that he might see something more within her and maybe connect the dots. She was really disappointed when he'd treated her the same as always, and in fact often seemed to be avoiding her even more than he'd done before. It was hard to have to stick to sneaking around, spying, and eavesdropping to know what was going on with him, and there seemed to be quite a lot going on with him. His poor head was all over the place—she could tell.

The day she'd had to pick him and Billie up from the pool had been super frustrating. She could tell something had happened but all Billie would say was that he'd had a bit of a dizzy spell and David himself wasn't saying anything at all. She had to listen at his bedroom door again to find out. Not that she wouldn't have kept up the vigil outside his room anyway. After she knew he had obviously experienced something bad, she wasn't going anywhere. He'd caught her there once but at least she'd managed to make it look as if she was newly arrived and had the excuse of asking him about his dinner. She'd managed to look after him that night in the way she wanted to, even if she did have to kind of force him into it. He'd looked so exhausted but so troubled that she decided to pop some of her herbal sleep remedies into his food just to give him a good night's sleep. She was sure he wasn't going to get any otherwise, and he obviously desperately needed the rest. Nothing bad would happen to him while he slept a deep slumber for a change, as she'd be there all night to look out for him.

When Billie went missing, Candy had pretty much given up hope of making any progress with David for that time being. All attention was focused on his lost friend. She got that, she only wished that she was closer to him prior to it happening so he could have confided in her and come to her for help. Of course, it had also made it a whole lot harder for her to do her job.

David insisted on wandering through the woods on his own looking for her and Candy was forced into following him. She knew she'd made mistakes that night and gotten too close to him. He heard her and was frightened but it couldn't have been helped. She'd felt he was in great danger that night and there was no way she was keeping the usual distance. He didn't see her and nothing bad had happened so it worked out okay. It was funny how her sense of doom had increased just before Andrew had turned up and couldn't explain why she'd instantly felt like attacking him the moment he'd stepped into view. He hadn't done anything wrong and had seen David safely back to the cars, but she couldn't shake the feeling that it had only happened that way because Andrew sensed he was being watched. For some reason, he gave her the creeps. She hadn't been at all happy to hear the two of them making plans to search the woods together the next day. She'd have to be there every step of the way. As such, it would be a waste of time cleaning her trainers. They'd only get dirty again so she left them in the garage. It wasn't as if anyone would pay attention to any of her stuff anyway. Apart from William, they all just tried their best to pretend she didn't exist so one pair of trainers wasn't going to be noticed.

She was ready and waiting the next day, an anxious knot in her tummy when Jill left leaving Andrew and David alone. That knot disappeared and she was overtaken by an icy rage when she heard the things Andrew was saying to David. She listened to him trying to bluff it out but Andrew wasn't buying it. He knew. Andrew was a Seeker and he intended to take David out.

She knew this was it. Whether David was ready to accept that she was going to be part of his life forever or not, whether he would despise her even more for it once he found out or not, she was going to have to act. He needed her.

She burst into the room and all the worries and hesitations about her and David's relationship flew from her mind. Seeing David being trussed up by a Seeker enraged her. In that split second, she not only learned what it really meant to be responsible for a Gatekeeper, she also learned how to trust her instincts. She'd known all along that something wasn't right about Andrew. She flew at him.

It felt really satisfying to kick his butt, but it felt even better to have saved her Gatekeeper. Frustrated that she couldn't get him free, she rushed from the room. Her face was flushed with embarrassment as she ran to her room to hunt down her scissors. How could she deal with a Seeker and not handle a bit of tape? Was that what she'd trained for all these years, just to fail at the simplest hurdle? She'd wanted David to be a little bit impressed, thought it might be a good start for a different relationship. Now she just looked like an idiot.

When she heard the almighty crash from downstairs, she knew she'd made a terrible, terrible mistake leaving David's side.

Luckily for her, Jill had things more or less under control by the time she arrived back downstairs. She was both incredibly relieved and incredibly jealous. Saving David was her job and this had been her first proper chance. It wasn't Jill's fault that she'd blown it, but part of her wanted to blame her anyway and divert the attention away from her own failings. No doubt Jen would assure her that she'd done well for her first time, and since everything had worked out all right, she should only learn from it and not dwell on it. It had been a real chance to prove her worth to David and possibly start building that relationship she really wanted, but it had slipped through her fingers. She told herself firmly that this was no time to try and deal with all the whirling emotions. This wasn't over yet. She still had a job to do. She needed to be calm, collected and detached.

~*~

Candy tried to stop her mind running over every second of their short journey so far as she stood on the sidelines in the massive warehouse. She wasn't thinking about the journey to get here; she was thinking of everything since the day she was assigned to David as his Watcher. She hoped it wasn't anything like when someone's life flashed in front of their eyes at the moment of their death, or if it was, then she hoped it was her's and not David's. That didn't seem likely since she'd been shoved aside as if she were of no importance and had to stand and watch her Gatekeeper face the danger without her.

She tried to keep calm, but inside, she raged and fretted. After the first day in the woods they'd spent together, she felt she'd finally made some sort of breakthrough with him. It wasn't massive, but maybe a tiny crack in the barriers he'd always had up against her. He hadn't had time to take in everything from the incident at school yet since they'd had to immediately head to this mission but he would, and she'd done much better this time. Sure, she'd still made some mistakes but she'd got there in time to save David herself and he'd seemed more thankful for her intervention than he'd been the first time. Then he'd asked her some serious questions, as if he actually trusted her knowledge and her judgement, as if he valued her opinion for once. Things were finally starting to turn around. She couldn't lose him now, she just couldn't. If anything ever happened to David, it would be the end of her as a Watcher. She would never trust herself with someone's life again. If she wasn't a Watcher, then she didn't know what she was. It was the only thing that had ever given her any sense of purpose or self-worth. It was everything and without it, she was nothing.

She was on the edge of interference as it was, only the sense in the coordinator's words about distracting the Gatekeepers keeping her on the edge of the action while her Gatekeeper battled without her. Those words held her pinned to the spot for a few seconds as she saw David being knocked to the ground. She silently screamed for him to get up, her fists clenched by her sides. Chaos exploded in front of her but she only had eyes for what was happening to David. She barely heard all the shrieks and desperate shouts. Then she saw the unthinkable.

She saw David give up and resign himself to his fate.

No! It was the only thought that raced through her head as she broke from the group of Watchers standing on the metaphorical outside and looking in. Let them obey if they wanted; she was done.

She had no idea what she was about to fight. She didn't care what it was or how terrifying it might be. The only thing that concerned her was her lack of perspective. Obviously, it was on top of David but she didn't know exactly where and she couldn't see how big it was. If she missed and went flying through thin air, it might be too late to help him by the time she recovered and gathered herself for another attack. Still, by the way, he was helplessly struggling and it looked heavy, so she had to assume it was pretty big. She had no more time to think and nothing to further judge it on anyway, so with her full speed gathered, she launched herself at her best estimation. The breath was knocked out of her as she hit it full on. The impact hurt but felt incredibly satisfying, especially when she realised she'd taken it completely by surprise and dislodged it from its prey. Her head spun as she clung on for dear life and tumbled over and over. No matter how dizzy she got, she wasn't letting go, wasn't giving whatever it was any chance to get back to David. As she came to a halt on her back, she felt it writhing and trying to twist in her arms. It was taking everything she had to contain it and she wasn't sure how long she could keep it up. Then she heard David's voice, felt a strong tug. This was different. It wasn't trying to break free; it felt as if it were being pulled away.

"Let it go, Candy. We've got it!" David said.

With him being so close, she was reluctant to comply, didn't want to put him back into danger and for her lucky break to have been in vain. Yet, for the first time, he sounded confident and in control. For the first time, it sounded as if they would actually be working as a proper team, and for the first time, it sounded like he might actually care what happened to her. She put her absolute faith in him and opened her arms, releasing the creature. Suddenly, it was gone.

She watched David take control over the entire situation as the other Watchers dragged her out of harm's way and out of the way of the Gatekeepers. She practically exploded with pride as he brought everything under control and she felt giddy with joy when he actually came over to check on her. Her injuries could have been a million times worse and they would've been worth it just for this moment, and that was before the one who'd been in charge before David took over came to give him some words of praise.

The chat they had on the way to the car and the grin they shared once in the car made Candy feel as if she was going to burst with excitement and happiness. Finally, she'd made the breakthrough she'd been longing for.

CHAPTER TEN

"Candy, this is a kid's game and it's stupid."

Candy looked at David with some sympathy. "I know it might feel dumb but there *is* a purpose to it, I promise."

"Then you'd better explain it to me 'cos I'm not playing anymore until you do. You're supposed to be teaching me to fight."

"Hush, keep your voice down. If Jill hears you she'll probably have me sent away, or throttle me with her bare hands."

"I don't know if she could do the second one, you've got some pretty good moves, ones that you're supposed to be showing me how to do I might add."

"I bet she could," Candy said with a giggle, ignoring the dig. "Nothing can beat a mamma bear who thinks something is threatening her cub."

David screwed up his face. "I'm not a baby bear, I'm a Gatekeeper, and it's time I started making my own decisions. Mum will just have to get used to that."

"Try telling her that."

"Well, maybe not yet," David conceded with a sheepish grin. "Could she really do that, though, have you sent away I mean?"

"I dunno, maybe. I don't remember hearing about a case where someone wasn't happy with their Gatekeeper, but I guess there's always a first time and no doubt if there was to be one, it would be me."

David toyed with the ball they'd been playing with, spinning it between his fingers and giving it the occasional small toss up into the air and catching it. "You know, you're strange. You always seem so confident on the outside, so sure of yourself, and you never let what anyone says get to you, shrugging it all off, but over the last few days I've seen a different side of you. Sometimes you're way too hard on yourself."

"You think?"

"Yeah. I wouldn't let anyone take you away. You're my Watcher and I'd fight for you."

Candy beamed. "Thanks, David. That really means a lot to me, but I bet you're only saying that because I agreed to teach you to fight."

"Maybe," David said with another grin, having learned to tease her a little. "But even though you agreed, you've got me in the back garden playing Donkey!"

"First off, we're limited in what we can do with Jill working in the kitchen. She can see out of windows you know. Secondly, there is a point to this. Don't take this the wrong way as it isn't meant to be an insult, but you've never been naturally sporty. I thought we'd better start with some of the basics like we did at the training academy. Okay, so we were a lot younger and it didn't feel silly to us but trust me, this is working on your hand-eye coordination and honing your reflexes. I'm starting you off easy and will build it up from there. The next stages will go much faster if you improve those skills in the beginning."

"Oh, okay then…I suppose."

"Great, so are you going to throw that ball or stand around all day?"

David reacted immediately, taking Candy by surprise by flinging the ball at her with all his might. She scrabbled to catch it, laughing as she dropped it.

"D!" he cried out triumphantly as she had to chase it down the slight slope of the garden.

~*~

Three weeks later, David had played more kid's games than he'd ever played in his life. Candy had him playing hide and seek, blind man's bluff, pin the tail on the donkey, and other games he considered nonsense that should be confined to parties for five year olds. She had him skipping, hopscotching, doing pat-a-cake, and some silly, girly, aerobics workout. This was stuff he hadn't even done with Billie when they were little. The only thing he did kind of enjoy, even though he would never admit it, was when they played sword fights with swords they made out of fallen branches they'd gathered in the woods. That was fun, even though he still felt a little foolish. Never before had he been so thankful for the privacy of their large back garden, and never had he missed his best friend more.

Throughout everything that had happened and every piece of torture Candy was putting him through before they got to the good stuff, Billie had never been far from his mind. He missed her like crazy and had never given up hope of her turning up back at home one morning as if nothing had even happened, or getting a call from her asking for his help. That was part of the reason he was willing to go through all this. If his friend needed him, then he wanted to be the best he could be in order to save her, and if Candy thought this was the best way, then he would put up with it for that reason alone.

Every night he sat on the edge of his bed and held the compass, staring at it and willing it to show him where she was, what direction he should take to find her. It always remained still, pointing due north stoically, and resolutely refusing to move. Every night he went to bed disappointed and hurting, and tonight was no different. No one else ever talked about her anymore. He knew they hadn't really forgotten but that was how it felt.

"Don't worry, Billie," he said in a quiet voice in the privacy of his bedroom. "I haven't forgotten. I'll never forget. We'll always find one another, remember?"

He tucked the compass under his pillow as he did every night and lay down. Every night he expected his head and heart to be too full to sleep but every night he found his eyelids drooping and himself drifting off within moments. The stuff he was doing after school with Candy must be doing more than he'd ever believed they could, they seemed to be pretty tiring. At least it was Friday night so there wasn't any school tomorrow and he could sleep in for a while.

It felt as if he'd only been asleep for about ten minutes when there was a sharp knock on his door.

"Time to rise and shine, David."

He opened his eyes groggily, seeing that his room was still dark. "I've only just gone to bed," he called back, grumpy at his slumber being disturbed.

A bright laugh came from the other side of the door. "Very funny. I'll give you ten minutes to shower and dress. If you're not in the kitchen eating breakfast in that time, I'm coming in there to get you. I've got a big day planned."

David looked at his clock, it was 5.30 am. He stuck his tongue out at the door but flung his duvet off. There was no point in arguing with Candy when she was in that bright and cheerful mood. She was more relentless then than when she was angry or disappointed. He went to shower as he'd been told.

Once he was dressed, he put his hand beneath his pillow to grab his compass. He always carried it in his pocket with him, no matter where he was or what he was doing. His fingers failed to touch upon its comforting shape no matter how much he groped around. Frustrated, he flung his pillows out of the way. There was nothing there. Frantically, he began to hunt all over the bed, ripping his duvet off to expose the entire mattress. When that didn't reveal it, he began looking on the floor around his bed. He was on his hands and knees peering beneath it when he heard a very familiar wheezy chatter behind him. He glanced over his shoulder, knowing exactly what he would see. The Hoogle sat on his desk, its mouth open wide in a drooly grin.

"What do you want? You'd better not have my compass," David said to the Hoogle.

David knew he would look utterly silly talking to the creature, even if he was observed by another Gatekeeper who could actually see the thing. It couldn't possibly understand what he was saying. After all, he'd never heard one talk and even if they did speak, they came from another dimension so there was nothing to say they would understand English, or any other language in the whole of this world for that matter. He was more surprised than annoyed when the thing held out one talon and there, dangling from the end of that long finger, was his compass.

He flipped round and sat on the floor, staring at it. "Did you understand me?"

The Hoogle chattered at him and waved its arm gently, causing the compass to swing on the short key ring chain.

David laughed at himself, shaking his head. "Of course it didn't understand you. It just knows exactly what it is you're looking for because it knows exactly what it took. Come on, game over, give it back."

He held out his hand, palm upright, moving his fingers in a 'give it here' motion. The Hoogle chattered and hopped from foot to foot. David watched, trying to assess what the thing wanted from him. Was it trying to tempt him over there so it could lead him on a merry dance, leaping out of his reach and teasing him with his possession? Or maybe it wanted to lure him into some sort of trap? The Hoogle had never hurt him before and he was no longer afraid of them, but they were incredibly mischievous and he wasn't sure just how far they would take their particular brand of trouble making to amuse themselves. Their idea of having some fun and his idea of fun might be completely different.

The Hoogle huffed and glowered at him, shaking the compass harder.

Talking to it had felt natural to him, like someone would talk to their pet, so he felt less ridiculous as he spoke again. "Okay, okay, I'll play along but this better not be some joke," David said sternly as he got to his feet and walked slowly over to his desk. "I don't have time for your games today."

He'd moved warily towards the Hoogle, half expecting it to leap away from him with those powerful hind legs then torment him again with his compass, holding it just out of reach. When it didn't move, he cautiously held out his hand. "Give it back, please."

To his utter surprise, the Hoogle dropped the compass into his hand then shot off, letting itself out of the room. He gave chase but by the time he got out into the hallway, the Hoogle had disappeared.

"What on earth was *that* all about?" he muttered to himself as he tucked the compass safely into his pocket. "It must have gotten bored with the game."

He shook his head, knowing it was unlikely he was ever going to make head nor tail of those things.

"David, you've got thirty seconds left to get down those stairs! Don't make me come and get you."

"Coming," David called back in answer to Candy's warning.

He hurried downstairs to join Candy in the kitchen before she made good on her threat. As he entered, he found that she'd laid a place for him at the breakfast bar with a bowl and spoon, and looked out the milk and his favourite cereal. The butter dish and the jam pot also sat on the table.

"I put the toast on as soon as I heard you on the stairs," she said. "It'll be ready in a sec. I want you have a good breakfast. Orange juice?"

"Please. So what was so important I had to get up even before the birds this morning?" he asked as he poured his cereal and added the milk to his bowl.

"Oh, I'm excited about this. I think you're finally ready!"

David's ears pricked up and he looked at her with equal excitement. "You're finally going to teach me some martial arts?"

"No, I think you might finally be fit enough to come on my run with me!"

"Your run? You practically drag me out of bed in the middle of the night and get me all hyped up and we're only going *jogging*?"

Candy looked offended as she brought him his glass of orange juice. "Hey, don't knock it unless you've tried it, and it's much more than jogging. I didn't use to just go for a little jaunt around the block."

"True, you used be gone for hours and hours. Why did you stop?"

"I had to after your birthday. I couldn't be away that long and you wouldn't have been interested in coming with me then. You wouldn't have been fit enough anyway."

"I might take offence at that," David said with his mouth full of cereal, "if I wasn't so certain it was the truth."

They shared a laugh and Candy felt a warm glow. They did that a lot more these days. "I'll tell you what, you make it three miles and we can stop in the woods and check on that weird place where your compass was going crazy before, just in case anything more has been happening there in the past couple of weeks. Also, if you think you've still got the energy, I can show you a few basic judo moves or throws there before we run home. How does that sound?"

"Exhausting," David said with a roll of his eyes. "I mean, three miles, come off it. I'll never make that."

"You'd be surprised how much fitter you are. I've been keeping track and all those silly little games as you called them that we've been playing have done wonders for your stamina. I bet you can do it."

"What are you willing to bet on it?"

"Anything you like," Candy replied with a shrug. "I'm confident in my abilities as a trainer."

"How about if I do it, you show me some judo moves and some really awesome karate moves, too?"

They grinned at one another.

"Yeah, you got yourself a deal!" Candy said, and they shook on it just as the toast went pop.

Chapter Eleven

Candy looked at David sprawled out on the forest floor and almost felt sorry for him. His hair was plastered to his head with sweat and his chest was heaving. She was sure that if he'd been standing, his legs would have been shaking. "You really shouldn't let your muscles stop cold; you'll risk damage or cramp. You need to do a gradual cool down."

"Can't," David gasped. "I'm dead."

"Well, at least let me do some stretches on you, like a physiotherapist or something would. I don't want to have to carry you all the way home."

"I think that's a very real possibility, even if…ow, that hurts!"

Candy knelt down and bent one of David's legs slowly until his knee touched his chest. "Don't be such a baby, it was only a little run. I told you that you could do it."

"I did, didn't I?" David said, beginning to recover and actually starting to feel a little pleased with himself. "Does that mean I get to learn how to do martial arts kicks?"

"Slow down there, Bruce Lee," Candy said. "Let's not kick before we can really run. Besides, I want to check out that weird place that we thought might be a gate. I still haven't heard of any strange happenings but if it is an active gate and nothing's come through yet, it'll be good practice for you to close it on your own. I tried to head in that general direction. Do you know if we're anywhere close?"

David extracted his foot from Candy's hand and sat up, looking around. "Yes, I think we are pretty close and I'm sure I'll be able to find it. There was a humungous tree right beside it. I've got my compass too so I can check and see if it goes haywire again."

"Great, come on. We'll take a brisk walk there and it'll count as a cool down."

Candy offered David her hand. He took it without hesitation. She couldn't believe how far they'd come in a few short weeks in terms of friendship. That major breach had been a real bonding experience for them. She reckoned it had gotten them to a place it might have taken several more months for her to reach without it. It was dangerous but turned out to be a blessing in disguise. She wondered if he felt that way too, or if he even gave it any thought at all.

"Oh, talking about the compass, you'll never guess what happened this morning."

She listened as David talked her through the incident with the Hoogle. He'd described those creatures to her in detail and she shuddered now as she pictured it. It might be a massive hindrance that she couldn't see the creatures from the other realms, but maybe it was another blessing too. The Hoogle sounded too disgusting even to contemplate. How David could stand them being that close around him she just couldn't fathom. "Any idea what it was playing at?"

"I was going to ask you the same thing."

"Sorry," she said with a shrug. "I haven't really got a clue. We didn't learn much about the creatures that come through; not our department. We know a little about the Hoogle because every Gatekeeper seems to encounter them frequently but not much, and even less about anything else. I think maybe that's deliberate. After all, we can't be afraid of what we can't see and don't know about can we? I could ask Jen next time I talk to her if she has anything on them she can give me, any report, or documentation that I didn't cover in basic training."

David nodded, knowing exactly whom she was talking about as he'd heard all about the woman who'd rescued her and mentored her. "That'd be great. I've got a feeling that the more we can learn about the Hoogle the better. Granddad won't tell me much more, saying I need to just concentrate on learning the mind control to push things back and shut the gates and that's all I should be focusing on. I'm not so sure, though, but don't ask me why. Oh look, I think that's the tree over there."

"It looks right." Candy looked back at him. "But did you bring the coordinates of the area so we can be sure?"

"Yes, they're still in my pocket here."

He was reaching into his jacket pocket for them as they made their way over to the large tree, but suddenly, he halted, a big grin spreading across his face. "I don't think I need them anymore, this is definitely the right tree."

"How do you know?"

"It seems to be home to about fifty Hoogle, and they're all looking at us right now."

Candy stared at the tree but could see nothing except the occasional rustle of some of the branches. From David's detailed description, she could picture it in her imagination, though. She gulped. "Are we safe, more importantly, are *you* safe?"

"There were just as many last time and they didn't hurt me. In fact, one came and sat on my arm so I'm sure we're fine. Come on; let's see if they'll interact with me again."

She wasn't sure about that but if she expected David to have faith in her, then she had to show absolute faith in him too. Trust was a two way street. She stayed close to his side as they stepped up in front of the tree.

"What exactly do you mean by interact with you, and why am I only hearing about this now?" Candy enquired.

"I didn't mention them last time because I didn't want to frighten you. I thought you might be a little overwhelmed if I told how many there were and what happened with that one."

Candy wanted to be furious with David for withholding information that might have been important but conceded that their relationship was different back then, still on very tentative footing, even it wasn't that long ago. David had obviously put the incident out of his mind or else he might have mentioned it to her. If he didn't consider it important then maybe she shouldn't either, but they were supposed to be a team. "Okay, well, thanks for being considerate enough to not want to scare me, I do appreciate that, but maybe you should tell me about that sort of thing in future. I do have a job to do here you know?"

She delivered her words in a playful manner, hoping that David took the point and not any offence. She didn't want him to think she was nagging him or telling him off. Although she was a lot older she didn't want to be like a parent or teacher, she wanted them to be more like friends and would only boss him around if his life depended on it.

Thankfully, he got the message in the spirit it was intended. "You're right. I'll keep you more in the loop from now on. I honestly just didn't think to mention it. It didn't seem important and I'd more or less forgotten about it."

"Fair enough. So what are the charming little Hoogle up to right now then?"

She watched David look up into the tree. "Not much, just kind of peering down at us."

"Do they look angry on annoyed that we're here? This could be their territory and we're intruding or something."

"I don't know. They have such weird faces, it's kind of hard to read any expression on them. I don't think so, though."

"Let me know if that changes any."

David laughed. "I will, I promise, if I can tell. I'm not sure I would know what an angry Hoogle would look like. Every time I've seen them before they've mostly been laughing at me, but I'll do my best."

"I'm not sensing that you're in any danger at the moment so I guess we're okay for now. Everything around here looks very peaceful. Can you see anything that might suggest the gate opened at any time and anything came through, any unusual prints, claw marks on the trees, anything like that?"

David hunted around a little but could find nothing to suggest that the serenity of the forest had been disturbed by anything not of this world. "Nope, it all looks good."

"Maybe we were wrong in thinking there was a gate here then. Oh hey, what about your compass, can you check it and see if it's behaving or not?"

"Um… I don't think I need to." David looked bewildered. "I know you can't see the disturbances in the light and air, but there's definitely a gate and it's about to open."

David dug his hand into his pocket, pulling the compass out and glancing at it just long enough to see the needle spin. He'd only quickly wanted to confirm his suspicions from last time. Whether all gates would make a compass do this he had yet to find out, but this one certainly did! Focusing his own attention back on the strange, shimmering light, he held the compass towards Candy for her to see.

She looked at it, seeing the needle go haywire. She glanced in the direction David was staring. "So we were right. How long have we got before the gate opens?"

"I don't know. I've only seen the whole process once before but if last time was anything to go by, moments at most, seconds maybe," he replied, tucking the compass away and bracing himself in front of where he knew by now that the strange, pulsating, glowing, shimmering white light would grow into a large circle and a gate would pop into existence where there had been nothing but woods before. The Hoogle on the tree had gone strangely silent. He risked taking a second to look at the tree, seeing them staring at the emerging gate with eyes wide and mouths open, almost as if in excited anticipation. There was a whoosh, a sucking sound, then a pop, and the gate was open. David peered through. "It's open," he said for Candy's benefit.

"What's beyond it?"

"A forest, pretty much the same as this one actually. If it wasn't for the shimmering around the entrance, I'm not sure I would even know I was looking through a gate."

"I've heard about that, that some of the other realms are closer to our own than others. The Realm considers these the most dangerous to the norms because if the air is breathable, the water is drinkable, and all the plants and animals look the same and stuff they assume that it would be safe for them, that they could live there, maybe colonise it, start over somewhere we haven't messed up, before they'd found out what else could be there."

"Like what they're talking about doing on Mars?"

She gave him a shrug. "I dunno."

"Never mind, I understand what you're saying."

"So can you see anything, any monsters?"

"No, only some birds in the trees and they look and sound pretty normal, too. You know, last time I was here I wondered if the Hoogle were gathered around waiting for the gate to open so they could go home."

"If that's what they're waiting for, then now's their chance. What are they doing?"

Now that nothing nasty had charged through the gate at them and it all seemed quiet on that other side, David could take the time to really study the Hoogle. Most of them had emerged from the deep branches of the trees, perching on the edge, while some had come silently down to ground level. All of them were still and quiet, as if poised, waiting for something. "They're not making any move to go through the gate anyway."

"Ouch! Something just bit me," Candy exclaimed, slapping at her neck. "I hate being out in the forest. Too many icky bugs."

David glanced back towards her. She saw his eyes go wide. "What? What is it?"

"Umm, I don't want to alarm you but turn your head very slowly and calmly and tell me if you can see anything," David said.

"Why?" she asked as she carried out his instructions, looking around her slowly. "I can't see anything."

"That's what I thought, but I really wasn't sure. I'm not sure if it's what bit you, but I know for certain now that the thing flying around your head isn't an ordinary bug. It must have come through the gate."

"Oh, Lord," Candy moaned. "Why does it have to be a bug of all things? I can handle anything but not otherworldly bugs. I can't even handle the ones here. I *hate* them. What does it look like?"

"Are you sure you want to know?"

"Now that you've told me about it, you're going to have to. It can't possibly be worse than what is in my imagination now anyway."

"Okay, well, it's not actually that scary to look at. It's pretty much like a cricket, but maybe three and a bit times bigger than normal, and it can kind of hover and dart about in a way crickets can't. I think the worst thing is that the buzzing of its wings is really loud and deep. Other than that, it really isn't that scary, honestly."

"That's fine for you to say, you're not the one it's after," Candy replied, rubbing at her neck. "That really hurt."

"Maybe it's looking to eat the normal little bug that bit you."

Candy wasn't sure if David was trying to reassure her or if he genuinely believed that. It helped anyway. She began to relax a little.

"Oh no, I was wrong," David said as he watched the thing hover beside Candy's exposed neck and a long proboscis with a needle sharp point extend from the cricket-like thing's mouth. "Candy, move quickly, and cover your face and neck if you can."

Candy squealed and leapt away. She pulled her t-shirt up over her neck to her hairline, then realised that it left her back and midriff exposed. Somehow, that seemed a whole lot worse. She pulled it down again. "Did I get away from it?"

"No, it's following you."

"Then send it back through! What are you waiting for you idiot!"

David focused his mind on the insect, preparing to do just that. Suddenly, a Hoogle was there, leaping up into the air with those powerful kangaroo-like hind legs, a long tongue flicking out of its drooling mouth. The loud buzzing went silent and was soon replaced by a satisfied crunching sound as the Hoogle munched on the bug. It swallowed deeply and gave a loud burp as it rubbed its tummy. It looked at David and huffed its laughter with an open mouth.

"You're okay, Candy. The Hoogle just ate it."

"Oh yuck, that's so gross!" Candy felt sick to her stomach but at least she felt a lot safer with the thing gone. "But thanks anyway, Hoogle."

She made her way back over to David and gave him a punch on the arm. "Way to go on the fast reactions we've been working on."

"Sorry. I get caught up in examining them. They're just so fascinating to see. I thought because this one didn't seem dangerous it would be okay to watch it for a while."

"That's exactly the kind of thing The Realm was talking about. You can't make those kind of assumptions. Besides, it really did hurt. Can you see anything on my neck?" She tilted her head to give David a clear view of the area that was still stinging.

"There's a huge red lump, like a mosquito bite or wasp sting, only bigger. I don't suppose you have any antihistamine on you? That might take the sting out of it."

"At home, but not with me," Candy replied. "I'll take some when we get back."

"Maybe a docking leaf would help, you know, like it does for nettle stings. Hang on; I'll see if I can find any."

David was so intent on his search that he didn't notice how far he was wandering away from Candy and the loud drone he could hear in the distance didn't really register. Once it did, he didn't give it too much thought. It sounded very much like a jumbo jet going past overhead and that was something he heard a lot so he barely noticed it. It was only when it grew really loud and sounded much closer than a jet ever should that he realised his mistake. He whipped round to look at the gate. All light from it and the view of the forest beyond had been completely blocked out by a huge black cloud—a loud, droning, flying cloud. It was a whole swarm!

"Candy! Run! Over here, as fast as you can."

She didn't need to be told twice and her 'fast as she could' was pretty fast by anyone's standard. She was by David's side in a flash.

David grabbed her arm. "Down behind this mound over here. Stay here, there's a massive swarm of them. I'm going to try and send them back and close the gate. Keep hidden and try to protect any exposed parts. Shout if you need me."

"What can I do to help?"

"Nothing, just keep safe."

David turned to rush back to the gate but the sight that greeted him halted him before he'd even got going. As the swarm of creatures burst through the gate and into this world, the Hoogle exploded into a frenzy. They were leaping into the air from the ground and the branches, their long tongues snapping out and pulling the insects in flight down into their waiting mouths with perfect precision, two, or three at a time, pausing only to crunch with expressions of bliss on their faces before starting the process all over again. It was absolute mayhem, but it was a beautifully coordinated mayhem that had David transfixed. Not a single insect was getting more than a few feet from the gate before it was brought down by a Hoogle, and the Hoogle looked as if they were having the time of their lives, battling one another to get to a specific insect they had in their sights, shoving and pushing, grabbing one another by the tails to hold them down on the ground, chuffing and puffing their huffing laughter.

Candy couldn't believe it when she heard David laughing. She peeked over the top of the rock covered with moss and fallen leaves where she'd been sheltering, seeing him standing there, laughing aloud at whatever it was he was seeing. She got up, brushed herself down with a disgruntled expression, and made her way over. "What's so funny?" She asked.

She couldn't help but giggle too when David described the scene to her. "I wish I could see it," she said through her laughter.

David continued to describe particularly humorous events to her until every last insect was gone and the woods were peaceful once more, on both sides of the gate. "The Hoogle are all just lying around now, hands on bloated bellies, looking really satisfied. There's lots of burping going on, though, and they think it's really funny."

"I'll let them off with the childish sense of humour since they just saved us from those nasty things. I guess you should go and close the gate now, though."

They made their way back over, David being careful to direct Candy so she didn't step on any of the Hoogle lounging around on the forest floor.

He was mentally preparing to close the gate when he suddenly had a thought. It wasn't a good thought either. It was one that sent his mind into a turmoil, his new Gatekeeper logic battling against the boy he'd been only a few weeks ago. "Candy, I need your advice on something."

Candy was absolutely thrilled, delighted that she would be the one he would turn to for help on anything, even though she didn't know what it was yet. "Sure, what do you need?"

"I need to talk something through so I can make sense of it. Will you stop me if anything I'm saying seems wrong to you?"

Candy chewed on her bottom lip. She didn't know about that. David was the smart one of the two of them and he'd never said anything that didn't sound like sense to her. "I can try."

"Good enough. I thought maybe the Hoogle had made their home in this tree as a temporary measure because they were waiting to go home. Yet the gate's open and they're all still here so that can't be it at all. With me so far?"

"Yes."

"So if I'm wrong on that, then there has to be another reason they hang around here in large numbers."

"Maybe they just like this tree…"

"Maybe, but it's a bit of a coincidence that it's one right beside a gate, especially when they all seem to want to stay here. That would mean that the gate has to be important to them for another reason, wouldn't it?"

"I suppose it would, but I can't see what use a gate would be if you didn't need it to go through."

"I think I might. You said you don't know much about the Hoogle but do you have any idea what they actually eat?"

"Not a clue, sorry."

"Okay, but we know that other Realms aren't always compatible with ours. What if the Hoogle can't eat anything in this world?"

"Oh! You mean like our plants and insects? Maybe they are poisonous to them."

"That's exactly what I'm thinking. If that's true, then they stay around here because those swarms are a guaranteed safe food source, meaning that they can survive here as long as the gate opens regularly and the insects appear. Am I making sense?"

"It sounds right to me, but then again, you can make anything sound right when it comes to the smart stuff."

"That's because I am smart," David teased, hoping to lighten the mood a little before he dropped his bombshell.

"And modest with it too," she teased back.

"The thing is, that leaves me with a massive dilemma."

"Which is?"

"That part of me is saying I should close the gate, but most of me is thinking that if we do then we cut the Hoogle off from their food supply. They might all die, and I don't know if I can reconcile myself with that. I should probably shrug and say they're only Hoogle, they're the ones trespassing in our world and no one wants them here anyway, but I just can't. I look at them and see intelligence there, despite their gross appearance. I know this might sound crazy, but I've come to feel quite affectionate towards them. I don't know if I can do anything that might harm them."

"So what is it you want to do?"

"I want to leave the gate open."

Candy chewed her lip again, looking worried. "I'm really not sure if I approve of that, David. The Hoogle took care of all the insects but what about anything else that comes through?"

"That's troubling me a little too, but there's no sign of anything else ever having come through. I don't know what to do."

"Me neither. I want to help but this is a big decision. Can't you talk to your grandfather?"

"I know exactly what he would say. He would tell me to close the gate."

"Well then, maybe you should."

"I can't. What if I kill the Hoogle for nothing? Maybe there's nothing dangerous beyond that gate. It obviously opens and closes fairly regularly and nothing bad has happened. Maybe there's nothing but plants, birds, and insects that the Hoogle take care of if they come through."

"And maybe it isn't."

"Maybe I should go and see for myself."

"No!" Candy exclaimed. "David, don't even say that, never mind think about doing it. You can never, ever go through a gate. Promise me you'll put that idea right out of your head and never think about it again."

"If you can tell me how we make this decision without facts, then I just might make that promise."

Going through a gate was the one risk she could never let him take. Besides, his instinct was telling him that leaving the gate open was the right decision, and they'd been next to it for a while now and she hadn't felt the slightest hint of danger either. Maybe it would be okay, at least for a little while. "I'll tell you what, why don't we leave it for now until I get the opportunity to speak to Jen about this. Gosh, I've got a million questions to ask her. I'll try and set up a meeting with her over the next couple of days, but we have to keep a really close eye on this place in the meantime, agreed?"

"Agreed," David said, giving her the brightest smile she'd ever seen from him. "Thanks, Candy, you're the best."

She couldn't have been more surprised when he hugged her. She hugged him back, pleased, but still concerned. "I hope we're doing the right thing. Come on; let's get home. My neck is stinging like a beast."

"We are, I'm absolutely sure of it."

She could only hope he was right.

CHAPTER TWELVE

"Granddad, what more can you tell me about the Hoogle?" David asked.

David's grandfather snorted. It was early Sunday morning and David, Candy, and his parents had come for a visit at David's request. Fearing his mother's reaction, he hadn't told her about his and Candy's decision to leave the gate open yesterday. In fact, knowing that she would ask lots of questions, he hadn't mentioned the gate incident at all. All he'd told her was that Candy had him jogging in the woods and then exercising in order to build up his strength, fitness, and stamina.

Jill hadn't exactly been thrilled at the idea of him being in the woods for hours with only Candy with him. She was struggling to come to terms with the fact that she of all people was David's Watcher. In Jill's eyes, she was just so… inadequate. As far as she was concerned, thc girl couldn't fight her way out of a paper bag. She intended keeping a close eye on her.

Still, although being a Gatekeeper was mostly about mental strength and ability, improving David's physical ability might help, especially if his Watcher wasn't really that capable of protecting him against Seekers. So, although she'd wanted to protest, she couldn't really find a valid reason to do so. In the end, she'd kept quiet about her fears and objections, but had maybe been a little less gentle than she might have been as she'd cleaned Candy's insect sting and applied an antihistamine cream. Served her right for being out in the woods when she wasn't equipped to deal with it, although she did seem to have had quite a bad reaction to whatever it was that got her. She'd held a fuss of course, but Jill hadn't expected much more from her; she held a similar fuss if she so much as had a ladder in her tights. She glanced at her now, sitting clinging to William's arm, a bright, vacant smile on her face. Jill idly wondered if she could maybe catch a moment alone with her father to discuss Candy with him today. Maybe there was someone high up she could appeal to, some way she could have the girl replaced with someone far more capable of protecting her son. Jill gave a deep sigh, knowing she was probably being unfair or too hasty, and it wasn't really in her nature to be either. She and Candy were becoming sort of friends before everything had happened so she felt mean and disloyal with the thoughts she was having. Still, this was David, her only child, her precious son, and his safety would always bring out her fiercest instincts. After a few more brief moments of soul searching, she decided she needed to give Candy the benefit of the doubt for now and just monitor the situation as she'd originally thought yesterday. With her decision made, she turned back to the conversation David was having with his grandfather.

"…they have some cognitive reasoning at least?"

"Yes, I suppose so," David's Granddad uttered. "In the same way a rat learns to navigate his way through a maze to get to the food or a squirrel figures out how to get into your house or raid bird tables. They're nothing but vermin, David, just a pesky nuisance that we could do without. The only decent purpose they serve is that they usually show up first, letting us know who is going to be a Gatekeeper and who isn't when they see them on their birthday. Because they aren't out to do any harm, they also ease them into this, getting them used to seeing these unworldly things and helping them be prepared before they come across something bigger and more dangerous. That's the only reason we put up with them. Now put those silly creatures out of your mind once and for all. Did you have any decent questions to ask?"

David couldn't help but feel disappointed. For some reason, he'd thought there was something more to the Hoogle, but if a seasoned Gatekeeper said there wasn't, then there couldn't be. He wouldn't press the point; he would only irritate his grandfather since he'd made his position on the matter so clear. It was time to ask his other burning question, but he would need to ease his way into it to distract Granddad from his earlier questions about the Hoogle. He didn't want him putting two and two together. "Yes. As Gatekeepers, if we're there in time, we see the gates open, as if they just pop into existence, but are they actually always there, even when they're not open and we can't see them?"

"Now that's a better question, and one that Gatekeepers have been asking for a very long time. We've come to the conclusion now that they're a permanent fixture, always there, but even Gatekeepers can't see them until they start to open. It's taken the Realm centuries of plotting intricate maps and recording patterns to be able to answer that one, but that's what we believe now. However, there must be thousands, maybe even millions that they don't know about yet and won't know unless they open and they learn of it."

"So can a gate be discovered by any way at all if it's not open or previously recorded, like say by sending a compass or something going haywire when close to it?"

"No, I'm pretty certain that couldn't happen. If that was the case, then all sorts of people would be reporting strange things going on with instruments all the time, and the Realm would have heard about it and put it to use by now."

That was what Candy had said, sort of. David glanced at her to see if she was giving him a smug look but she was too busy examining her buckled and studded boots, turning one foot this way and that to admire it from different angles. In light of what had happened with his own compass, he continued questioning his grandfather in hopes of finding an answer and making sense of it all. "Maybe the Realm just hasn't heard about it yet."

"Impossible. They keep a pretty close ear to the ground. There's little that happens with the gates that they don't know about."

David gulped, wondering just how much trouble he would be in if they found out or already knew that he'd left a gate open on purpose. This time, when he turned his head towards Candy, he was in time to see her flick her eyes in his direction, but she quickly looked away again before he could catch her eye and allow any silent exchange to pass between them. He pushed the thought from his mind, as it seemed to be the right time to ask the big question. "So what would happen to a gate if it opened somewhere obscure and no one ever saw it and it never came to the Realm's attention?"

"Nothing would happen to the gate itself. It would just sit there open, close again come time, then open again when it was ready. It's the absolute chaos it would cause in the meantime that would happen, all manner of things crossing in both directions. There's no telling where that would lead."

David ignored the last part of what his grandfather said. Not only was it not what he wanted to hear, but the first part was too exciting. He perched on the edge of his chair, his face animated. "They do that, open and close on their own without intervention?"

"They do."

"How often? What sort of time scale are we talking about?"

"That's where it gets tricky. Each one is different. I think the shortest recorded opening I've heard of was three hours, but that's still too long, a lot can happen in three hours."

"What about the longest?"

"Well, that isn't on record because if we know about a gate, it gets closed by us and that's the end of it until it opens again."

"How long does that take, how often does the same one open?"

"That's something else that differs for each individual gate. It can be days, weeks, or years and years. Some on record have never opened more than once and when they're closed, they seem to stay closed, or at least so far anyway. They're complex things, highly unpredictable. It's why we have to stay so vigilant at all times. I'll tell you a little story, though. There are some gates that we know must be in existence but they can never be found. You've heard of the Loch Ness Monster, haven't you?"

"Up in Scotland, of course, everyone's heard of Nessie, but it's just a local legend, isn't it? She doesn't really exist."

His grandfather gave him a knowing look and a wink.

"No way!" David cried. "Are you telling me Nessie is real, that she's something that came through a gate? I thought all the photographs and everything had been proved hoaxes and that the loch had been extensively searched and no sign of her had ever been found."

"That's all true but just because the so called proof has been pronounced fake doesn't mean to say that the monster is. People were talking about sightings long before anyone was able to take such a thing as a photograph."

David had been avidly listening to the story, enjoying it immensely, but now he realised that something wasn't adding up. "You're pulling my leg, aren't you? This doesn't make any sense. Only Gatekeepers would have been able to see Nessie and they certainly wouldn't have spoken about it to anyone because of how important it is that they keep the secret, so they certainly wouldn't have made her into the phenomenon she is now. She attracts far too much attention."

"That's what so fascinating about this particular tale. You see, David, sometimes, when a gate closes again, quite quickly, things can get stuck on this side, in our world."

David was agog. He hadn't even thought about that part yet. His head was alive with questions but knew when it was best just to let his grandfather go into his story telling mode and not interrupt. He would get more information that way so he stayed quiet, silently willing him continue.

"Something strange seems to happen when creatures spend a lot of time in our world. Even the Realm can't explain it, and all their great scientists have been working on it for years but haven't come up with any definite. It might be because of living in our atmosphere, eating the food, drinking the water, or even just the very vibrations of our world itself, but if they're here for long enough without crossing back to their own world, they start to become visible, to everyone, not just Gatekeepers."

His grandfather stopped talking, giving the information time to sink in. It had come as a massive revelation to David and his mind was filled with every legendary monster that he could remember, from sea serpents to abominable snowmen. Could it be possible that they were all things that had come through gates and gotten stuck here?

His thoughts must have been obvious because old Geoff was nodding at him. He continued, "It's why it's so important to close the gates quickly before anything comes through and to make sure everything is sent back before we do. Sometimes we might be able to deal with a creature in other ways but it's not a good plan. Evidence left behind always has a way of being found, no matter how careful you are."

"I understand," David said, getting that part without any further explanation. "But can we go back to Nessie for a moment. Did the Gatekeepers close the gate while she was still on this side?"

"No, that's what I started out telling you about, wasn't it? I must have gotten a little side tracked. Nessie's gate was never, ever found. We missed it, and so must she. The Realm assigned a team to keep watch but no one ever saw it open again. It must be somewhere in the actual Loch itself, and at twenty-three miles long, a mile wide, and nearly eight-hundred feet deep, Loch Ness is an impossible search area to keep a watch on, especially underwater. It just can't be done, and if we can't find the gate, we can't send Nessie back through and close it again. But considering the first sighting was reported back in the 7th century, the gate must have opened and closed a few times by now at the very least."

"So that could explain why she hasn't been found when divers have gone down and they've dredged the Loch and stuff!"

"It could. We have no way of knowing when the gate is open and when it isn't. All we know is that if she chooses to go back at times, she's never back for long enough to negate the effects of becoming visible here for long, and she always chooses to come back."

"Wow, that's amazing. I've certainly learned a lot about the gates and how they work. Thanks, Granddad, it's been fascinating talking to you."

Geoff looked pleased. "No problem. That's what I'm here for. How are you getting on with the mind exercises I gave you?"

"Good, I think. I do them every night like you told me to and I don't feel as if I'm finding them difficult. Putting them to use would be the only way I'd know for sure, though."

"I know you're going to do great, my lad. You are my grandson after all."

"Well, on that note," William said, stretching. "My stomach's telling me it must be nearly lunchtime. How about we all go out for a nice Sunday lunch? I've heard they do a very good carvery at The Red Dragon. Who fancies it?"

"That sounds great!" Candy enthused.

"Mum, Dad, do you fancy it?" Jill asked.

Betty, David's grandmother, had been sitting very quietly throughout her husband's conversation with David. Now she was quick to answer in her soft voice. "Oh, thank you, dear, but I think we'll pass. I'm not dressed for going out and it all seems like such trouble. Besides, I took a small joint out to defrost last night. You're all welcome to stay here for lunch, I'm sure we can make it stretch with plenty of trimmings."

"Oh no, we couldn't possibly put you out any longer since we all turned up unexpectedly as it is," Jill replied Betty. "I know you wouldn't put your feet up and let me do it all, so absolutely not. Why not come out with us. You look absolutely fine, very nice in fact."

"No, no. If I'm honest, I really look forward to small things like a Sunday roast with Geoff. It's only recently that he's stopped having to be tearing off at a moment's notice with no idea of when he'll be home. It's nice to be able to guarantee we can get through a meal without him being called away and me worrying like mad. You go out and have a nice time, and I'll have just as good a time here preparing a special meal that I know he is going to get to enjoy."

"I understand. Can I help before we go?"

"No, off you go, go on, shoo, go and get a table before the place is full up and they run out of food."

"Okay, okay," Jill said, laughing at her mother's insistence. "We're going. Come on everyone; let's get out of their hair."

Goodbyes were said all round and Jill, William, David, and Candy piled into the car. William drove away while David waved to his grandparents standing in the doorway until they were out of sight.

CHAPTER THIRTEEN

"I won't know what to choose," David said as the four of them walked down the street towards the pub that was rapidly gaining the reputation of having the best carvery in town. "Not if they have beef *and* gammon joints."

William ruffled his son's hair. "Well, since we parked in the multi-story and it's a bit of a walk, you'll be walking it off on the way back to the car, so why not just ask for a couple of slices of everything they have. That way you don't have to agonise over the decision."

"That sounds terrific, but I'd be worried they might charge you extra for that."

"I think I could stretch to it," William said, barking out a laugh. "Besides, you deserve it. You've had a lot to deal with recently, we all have. A good afternoon out is just what we all need. Maybe if your mum agrees to drive home I could even have a pint."

David didn't know it just then, but that's what would stick in his mind for such a long time to come. How it was such a nice, pleasant conversation with all of them looking forward to a slap up meal and his Dad looking forward to maybe having a beer for a change. None of them could possibly know that their plans were going to turn upside down in a heartbeat.

It was Candy who knew something was wrong first, turning to David with wide eyes and clutching at his arm. "Seekers!" she hissed at him.

She looked around frantically, trying to find somewhere that would offer him some safety. There was nowhere. Being Sunday, all the small, independent shops on this street were closed. They were a long way from the large shopping centre filled with chain stores that would be open and bustling with people, and the pub they were heading to was down at the other end of the street. They wouldn't make it; the Seekers were too close. She couldn't risk sending David off there on his own while she held them back in case there were more of them further on. Besides, she also had William and Jill to think about. This assessment only took her a few seconds. All her synapses firing in the face of danger, every part of her brain doing what she'd been born to do. In the end, she shoved David towards his parents and pressed them all back up against a shop doorway, taking up a fighting stance in front of them just as three people burst out of a car that had stopped at the traffic lights just ahead of them.

"Candy, what's going on?"

William, the least immersed in this strange life was completely bemused but Jill, realising something bad was happening, grabbed David and shoved him behind her then seized her husband's arm and pulled him in close to her so that they created a human shield in front of David. She despaired over the fact that there wasn't much else she could do. By the time she'd done this, the fastest of the three had already reached Candy. Jill could only watch with horror as the events unfolded in front of her. William made a move to rush forward but David grabbed him to stop him.

"Don't worry, Candy can take care of this," David said with absolute confidence. "You'll only get in her way."

The man had launched himself at Candy with a martial arts style kick, flying through the air at her with leg extended. Normally, she would have dodged it easily, having read his intent and seen it coming, but if she did that, then he would hit Jill or William behind her. Not only would he do them serious injury, but it would give him a clear path to his target—David. She had no choice but to stand her ground. A split second before impact, she reached up, grabbed his ankle, and twisted as hard as she could. She still took the full force of his weight flying through the air and it sent her staggering backwards, but William's strong hands were there to catch her and right her, lending his strength to her for that brief moment to halt the human projectile, while Candy's twist on his leg disrupted his carefully balanced flight and sent him crashing to the ground at her feet. She grasped handfuls of his clothing and yanked him up, using him like a bowling ball as she flung him outwards towards the other man and the woman that were just reaching them. He hit the woman and she staggered, the two of them falling to the ground in a tangled heap, giving Candy a precious time advantage to deal with the other man. Already in close quarters to her, and with the three she needed to protect still behind her, she didn't have much room to work with. When she launched a volley of short, sharp boxing jabs, she took him by surprise. Her first punch caught him on the chin, the next on his nose; by the third punch, he was expecting it and ducked his head so it glanced off his right cheek.

Just at the moment that he leered at her through the blood streaming from his nose and raised a meaty fist to hit back, she popped out a foot encased in a spike-heeled, pointed toe, boot and hooked it behind his ankle. With one jerk of her leg, his leg disappeared from beneath him and he fell, landing heavily on his backside. In normal life, Candy would never kick a person when they were down but this was a Seeker, and there were no rules or morals when it came to protecting her Gatekeeper, not to mention the man she loved. She drew back that pointed toe and released all her fury with a little jump before her swing, then she did it again, and again, enraged that their perfect Sunday had been interrupted. She caught him in the stomach several times, and finally, in a man's most sensitive place, which had him curled up into a ball and howling in agony, tears streaming from his eyes. He wasn't getting up in a hurry.

While Candy was dealing with him, the other two had untangled themselves. The woman had hit the back of her head hard on the pavement and was dazed, the other man had paused to check on her, once more buying Candy the valuable time to deal with the second attacker. Now the two of them were on their feet and advancing on her. She'd obviously twisted the man's ankle as he was limping. A swift kick to his knee on the opposite leg dropped him to the ground. With a bad ankle on one side, and a kneecap screaming in agony on the other, he wasn't going to be getting up too quickly either. That left the woman to deal with, and Candy knew she might be the most dangerous of them all.

Using her brains instead of her brawn, she made as if to circle Candy, hoping she would follow suit and step away from where Jill and William were shielding David. Candy refused to bite, simply holding her position and moving her head to keep an eye on her, watching for clues for what she might try when the inevitable attack came. She knew it wouldn't be a head on attack the same as the men had tried. Women tended to be sneakier fighters and would use a whole lot of dirty tricks, while men relied on their brute strength.

Candy was right. The woman ran at her but at the last minute dropped low and shot out a leg, trying to trip Candy as she'd done to the first attacker earlier. Candy had read the move and had jumped aside as far as she dared without leaving her charge exposed, but the tip of the woman's toe caught her and she stumbled a little as she landed. Her assailant took advantage, leaping onto her back and wrapping her legs around her chest, crossing them at the ankles to cling on. She tried to reach around to scratch at Candy's eyes with one hand, hanging on with an arm around her neck with the other. Candy whipped her head back and forth, shaking it wildly so the woman couldn't gouge her fingers into her eye sockets as she was trying to do, her long, blonde hair flying everywhere. The woman changed tactics, grabbing handfuls of it and yanking hard.

For the first time, unable to see due to the tangle of hair in front of her eyes, Candy risked stepping away from David, moving so that she could run backwards and slam the woman on her back against whatever was behind her. It happened to be a large, shop front window, which shattered with a deafening crash as the two of them hit it with force. Glass rained down upon them as they fell backwards through the ruptured window. Candy heard a sickening thud as the woman's head connected with a window display unit and the arm around her neck and the legs around her waist went limp. Her attacker had been knocked out cold.

Lying on her back on top of the third Seeker, Candy looked around for a place to put her hands down to push herself up. Everywhere was covered in splinters of broken glass. Suddenly, William was there, holding out his hands for her to take. He pulled her to her feet and into his arms, hugging her tightly.

"That was the most terrifying thing I've ever had to stand and watch," he told her. "Are you okay?"

Candy hugged him back then extracted herself, knowing she still had to keep an eye on all three

Seekers. Any one of them could recover enough to make a move on David at any moment. "A few cuts from the glass, other than that, I'm fine," she assured him. "Bring David in here and see if you guys can find anything to tie them up with while I make a quick phone call. Anything will do, but the tape would be best."

Candy dug her phone out of her pocket, hoping it hadn't been broken in the fight. It was intact and working, and this time she had the number of the clean-up crew programmed into one of the speed dial slots. She'd had the feeling she was going to need them a lot. A hurried conversation with them to give her location and to tell them it involved Seekers was all that was needed. They didn't need to ask any questions. They would come prepared to handle any situation.

Within moments, they had all the Seekers tied up and had dragged them inside the shop, hopefully to keep them away from prying eyes. They were all glad it was Sunday and that the street had been quiet. Anybody that had seen anything from the odd passing car had probably assumed it was a domestic fight and had averted their eyes and driven on, not wanting to get involved.

"Right, you three get out of here," Candy said to David and his family. "The window might be alarmed and if the police arrive before the Realm gets their clean-up crew here, things could get very messy and complicated. You'd be better off not being around. I'll wait here and deal with whatever happens next."

"No way are we leaving you," David said. "Not when you've just saved my life again."

"You'd better get used to that, it's what I'm here to do, and it's no big deal for me," Candy replied.

"She's right," Jill said. "This is her job and we can't be sentimental about that. We should get David out of here."

"She might be David's Watcher but she's also my girlfriend and I can't not be emotional or sentimental or whatever about that. I'm not leaving her," William said emphatically.

Outnumbered, Jill had to concede, even though every instinct was screaming at her to get David away from this place, away from the danger that was lying bound and gagged only feet away. She didn't have to worry about it for long. A big, black van pulled up outside the shop front and four people in the familiar, garish uniforms leapt out. They took seconds to take in the scene, then addressed Candy directly.

"Okay, we'll handle everything from here. Get your Gatekeeper out of here." Those were the only words uttered as they turned to get to work.

"See," Candy hissed to David, William, and Jill as they stepped across the broken glass and vacated the shop through the non-existent window. "I told you to go. Now they think I'm an idiot."

"I don't care what they think," William said, draping an arm around Candy's shoulders. "I thought you were absolutely magnificent and I couldn't be more proud of you."

"Thanks," Candy said with a giggle, blushing furiously.

"So, does anyone still feel up for lunch?" William asked hopefully.

"Oh heavens, no!" Candy exclaimed. "That awful Seeker was pulling my hair; I must look an absolute fright! I have to get home before someone I know sees me looking like this, or anyone for that matter."

Chapter Fourteen

Candy knocked gently on David's bedroom door and waited until she heard him call out for whomever it was to enter. She opened it a fraction and poked her head around. "All right if I come in for a minute?"

David was in his pyjamas and tucked up in bed, his side light on and a book in his hand. He popped his bookmark in to keep his place before closing it and laying it aside. "Come on in."

Candy closed the door behind her when she entered, taking a seat on the bed when David scooted over to make room for her in a silent invitation.

"I just wanted to check on you before bed," she said. "Make sure you were okay after today."

"It's me that should be asking you that."

"I'm absolutely fine. Jill patched me up again pretty well. She'll probably get tired of doing it but I'm grateful anyway. She always takes care of me. She even brought me a cup of camomile tea. She's so nice."

"Not always. She wanted us to leave you remember?"

Candy smiled at David. "Well, sure, but I understand that. Being a Gatekeeper is an amazing thing, a privilege even, just like being a Watcher is, but it also comes with a lot of responsibility and danger. Jill obviously knows and understands this crazy life we lead but you've got to remember that she's your mum. To her, that other life is always going to be more important. You'll always be her son first and a Gatekeeper second. She'll put you before everyone and everything else and protect you in a different way than you'd maybe want, but that's just the way it is and the way it has to be, and I'm thankful for that. You should be, too."

"Please don't get me wrong, I love Mum very much and I'm grateful for the way she accepts this. It's just that sometimes I feel she holds me back a little. I could have done something to help today; instead, I just hid behind her skirt tails."

"That's exactly what you should be doing in those types of situations," Candy said firmly. "You're far too important to risk your life like that. I'm replaceable; you're not. Don't ever forget that. I promised I would teach you to fight but it's only for an absolute emergency, like say if something happens to me and you have to protect yourself. If you can't promise me that you'll always take the safest option first, I'll have to change my mind about teaching you anything. Can you promise me that you'll always run if you can run, hide if you can hide, and keep yourself safe no matter what the cost?"

It wasn't a promise David wanted to make. He hated the idea of standing back and seeing Candy or anyone else he cared about get hurt, but it seemed to be a promise she desperately needed to hear and so he made it, and not just so she would still teach him to fight. He made it because he knew it would upset her if he didn't.

"Yes, I promise."

She smiled at him. "Thank you. Now we can move on to the other thing that I really wanted and came in to talk to you about. That was some really interesting stuff Geoff was saying about the gates today, stuff I had no clue about before, but it did make me worry about the decision we made yesterday."

"It made me a bit worried too, but I think it also proved that I was right. That gate opens and closes, and every time it opens, it feeds the Hoogle. We had to be right in leaving it alone. Maybe it wouldn't open again for a much longer time if it had been closed by a Gatekeeper and they would have all starved."

"It's all so confusing sometimes," Candy said with a sigh. "There always seems to be so many questions and whenever we do get an answer to anything it only makes a million more questions come up. Trying to figure it all out makes my head hurt."

"I know what you mean. I can't work through half of this stuff either. The hard facts just aren't really available for me to apply any logic to it. Still, Nessie's gate has been open for centuries and that hasn't done anyone any harm…"

"That's maybe just because she's a shy, retiring, vegetarian who just wants to live a quiet life and stay out of the public eye."

"Maybe, or maybe it means that there isn't anything dangerous to humans on the other side of that gate."

"It would be wonderful to think so, wouldn't it? That there are other worlds we can safely explore and allow all the species of animals of roam back and forth and breed and make up brand new types of animals and things, but the Realm have to know what they're talking about and if they say it's too dangerous for anyone to ever go through or for a gate to be left open then I guess we have to listen. After hearing your granddad talk today I'm starting to think we did the wrong thing in leaving that gate open."

David's expression changed from thoughtfulness to one of panic. "Candy, please! I know Granddad said a lot of unflattering things about the Hoogle and I know he's got years of experience and is far more knowledgeable than we are, but for some reason, I've just got a gut feeling he's wrong and that there's more to the Hoogle than what I see on the surface or what anyone else thinks about them. Please don't make me close that gate, please. Not yet anyway. At least, give it a fair chance to see what happens. I promise I'll deal with whatever happens and take the blame if we get caught. I'll close it the minute it starts to look dangerous in any way, I swear!"

Candy heard the desperation in David's voice and saw the pleading on his face. How could she possibly refuse him this one thing when he asked her for so little? He was being an absolute trooper about the way he was handling everything, especially since he was still essentially the shy, quiet, studious boy he'd always been and was struggling to find his way through all this. "Yeah, okay, but only for now so we can assess the situation. The minute it looks like something bad might happen, it gets closed, agreed?"

"Absolutely," David said. "Thanks, Candy, and thanks again for today. You were ace."

Candy blushed. "I don't know about that but thanks anyway. I've got a feeling it's going to be happening more often, though. The word seems to be getting around the Seekers about you now and since those have failed, there might be bigger and bigger groups coming to try and get to you. We both have to be on our guard at all times. They know you're a gatekeeper now and they seem to know you're something just a bit special. They'll stop at nothing."

"I should really be worried about that I know, and I will be on my guard and not trust anyone, but somehow, I can't be that worried while I have you. You make me feel safe," David said, snuggling down into his pillow and yawning.

Candy couldn't have been more pleased. Seeing that he was ready to sleep, she rose and tucked his duvet up around him. "Maybe, if your parents agree, we can all take a trip to Scotland sometime and see if we can see the Loch Ness Monster. It would be so cool to see a creature from through a gate for a change. Sweet dreams, David."

"That would be fun, I'd like that. Night, Candy."

He was already half asleep, his words mumbled. She turned off his light and tiptoed out of his room, closing his door gently behind her. She'd managed to reassure David, now she had to go and face William, who no doubt would have plenty of things to say to her about the danger she was in doing what she did. She could really do without the lecture tonight but knew that he'd need to talk it over. She sighed. It was such a pity that he'd had to witness it first-hand but she supposed he was bound to find out sooner or later. She might as well face it now and get it over with so they could all go to bed happy.

CHAPTER FIFTEEN

It had been four days and from Candy's perspective, everything had been quiet, no calls to gates, no Seekers, nothing. She'd had that long talk with William and although he maybe hadn't completely come to terms with what she did, he understood that she desperately needed to be a Watcher, and he would only offer her support and enthusiasm from now on and not burden her with his worry for her. That was only a small part of why she loved him so much.

Jill too had approached her, asking for a quiet word. She'd explained to her the doubts she'd had about her ability as a Watcher, then went on to say that she was highly impressed with the way she'd protected all three of them on that awful Sunday. She'd said that she understood now that Candy would lay her own life on the line for David, and that was all anyone could ask of a Watcher, and all a mother could ever ask for her son. The two women had a deeper mutual understanding of one another after the talk and they'd hugged at the end of it, a closer bond now formed between them, negating some of the awkwardness of the living situation. Candy had been pleased with the outcome of the conversation and hoped it would make life a lot easier for all of them to be under the same roof all the time.

Other than that, nothing much had been happening. She and David had checked on their secret gate every day after school but it had been closed every time they'd arrived and none of the Hoogle that lived in the nearby tree had been showing any interest in it so they'd assumed it wasn't about to open again anytime soon. They'd also advanced his training a little, with Candy working on both his physical fitness and the mental state of mind required for martial arts. It was slow progress but he was coming along nicely, all things considered. This period of inactivity with no threat to David should have made her happy—but it didn't. For reasons that she couldn't explain, it put her on edge. She couldn't help thinking that it was the calm before the storm, that something very bad was bound to happen soon.

From David's point of view, things hadn't been quite as quiet, although nothing bad had been happening. The Hoogle had most definitely become an increased presence in his life, though. It wasn't in any major way, he just seemed to see them a lot more frequently. He would waken in the morning and maybe find one in his room looking down at him as he slept, or he would go down into the kitchen and see one sitting on the counter, or maybe even glance out of the window in one of his classrooms and see one looking in. If he were forced to explain it, he would have to say that it was almost as if they liked to be around him for some reason. He had no logic to base that on so would never voice it aloud to anyone, but it was the way it felt to him. If he happened to be alone and had total privacy then sometimes, he would chat with them the way someone might talk to their cat or dog, not expecting them to pay any attention and certainly not expecting any reaction. He never even knew if it was the same one or a different one each time; they all looked the same to him. Still, it would seem rude to ignore them completely so he didn't. Occasionally, one would cock its head slightly at something he said, but that was the most interaction they ever offered. At least they'd mostly stopped stealing things now, or certainly, the things belonging to him. He couldn't help but chuckle whenever Dad couldn't find his keys or the T.V. remote, or Mum was hunting high and low for a certain top or skirt she wanted to wear and couldn't find it anywhere. He was finding that whenever he misplaced something it would turn up fairly quickly, and always somewhere he would look first so he couldn't blame the Hoogle for those incidents. All in all, with school, the Hoogle, and everything he was doing with Candy, David's life was pretty full and he didn't have much time to think about the fact that things had been very quiet recently.

It was the following Tuesday that everything changed.

David was in his history class, listening to his teacher talking about the Jacobite rebellion and trying not to let his mind wander to his grandfather's story about Nessie and her gate when a sharp knock at the door had everyone sitting up with interest and paying more attention than they had during the actual lesson.

"Come," the teacher called.

One of the school secretaries entered, carrying a note that she handed to the teacher. He scanned it briefly, a concerned frown crossing his face. When he looked up, he looked straight at David. "David Edwards, please accompany Miss Strachan to the head teacher's office."

David's heart sank. Getting called to the head teacher's office usually meant you were in trouble of some kind, although he couldn't for the life of him think what he'd done. Of course, it was no longer Froggy Ferguson that was running the school, he was long gone, carted off by the Realm to goodness knew where. The school now had a headmistress instead of a headmaster—a lady called Mrs. Duff, whom David had so far found he liked. She seemed firm, but fair, and seemed to command the respect she needed to as well as be a sympathetic and understanding ear when necessary. It was a good mix, and she also gave her students plenty of encouragement to succeed. David considered her very good for the school and being called in to see her was a lot less frightening than being called in to see Mr. Ferguson. Still, being called in to *any* head teacher's office was never a good thing.

He was still wondering what he'd done as he walked through the quiet corridors with Miss Strachan. When he caught her casting him a sympathetic glance, his thought pattern began to change and he began to worry. Was something wrong? Had there been a family emergency of some sort? He was on tenterhooks by the time he got to the office. His feeling of dread only grew when Mrs. Duff also greeted him with a warm, sympathetic smile and a look of pity on her face.

"Ah, David, come on in and take a seat for a second," Mrs. Duff said.

David did as he was asked and Mrs. Duff waited until he was settled before she spoke. "I'm afraid I have some bad news for you. It would seem that your mother is not very well. Don't panic, I'm certain that all will be well and she's certainly in the best place as she's been taken to the hospital. A family friend, a…" Mrs. Duff paused to look down at her notes. "…Candy Peterson is waiting right outside to take you there now. Don't worry about your things, we'll gather them and have the janitor put them in your locker for you, and you can collect them whenever you return. Are you ready to go?"

David had turned pale at the mention of his mother being ill, his hands gripping the arms of the chair he was seated in until his knuckles turned white. However, at the mention of Candy, he began to wonder. Surely, if his mother was ill, then it would be his father who would have come for him and he would want to break the news to him himself. He suddenly had a sneaking suspicion that this wasn't a family crisis after all, but Gatekeeper business. He certainly hoped so. He nodded in response to his headmistress's question, knowing that if it was a ruse, he needed to play along and keep up the pretence of being very concerned. Him not knowing, either way, made that very easy.

Mrs. Duff escorted him to the large double doors of the school and held one open for him to pass through. He saw Candy sitting in her car outside, not looking in their direction.

"Take as long as you need, dear, but please ask your father to keep us informed."

"I will," David said, hurrying down the steps and leaping into the car. He waited until Mrs. Duff had gone back inside before he spoke, busying himself with fastening his seatbelt in the meantime. "Is there anything really wrong with Mum?"

"No, she's fine, but we've had an emergency call about a gate."

David breathed a massive sigh of relief. "Gee, Candy, did you have to worry me that way?"

"I'm sorry," she said, already pulling out of the school car park. "I couldn't think of anything else that would actually get you out of school."

"Is this going to happen a lot?"

"The gates don't open to fit around a timetable and if we're called to an emergency, then we have to go, no matter what. That's another reason why I thought it might be a good idea to have a cover story of a parent not keeping in good health—so we can use it whenever we need to."

"Great, Mum's going to love that. She'll think it's like tempting fate or something."

"Then we'll come up with something else to use next time. It really was the best I could do at short notice."

"Fair enough, but I'd rather not use it again. What's happening anyway?"

"A gate has opened right in the middle of the shopping centre in town. Everyone who can get there quickly has been called and word has been sent to others who can't arrive until later. It's a big one and, of course, the place is full of staff and shoppers. We're going to be one of the first teams on the scene I would imagine. Hold on tight, I'm going to have to drive fast. This is about as drastic as it can get."

Candy hadn't been kidding about her driving. She weaved and bobbed through the traffic, jumping lanes and barrelling through amber lights, pushing every boundary when it came to the Highway Code and taking chances that on occasion made David screw up his eyes as he was afraid to watch. He thought it was a miracle that she managed to get them to the large, multi-storey car park in one piece, and even more of a miracle that she parked up safely after taking all the ramps and tight turns at high speed. He was trembling when he got out of the car, half thinking that he never wanted to experience that again, and half wondering if she would teach him to drive when he was old enough. It might have been frightening, but it *had* been cool too. One thing he could say for certain; it had kept his mind off what he might have to face at the shopping centre. Now that thought was all that consumed his thoughts.

"Which floor do we need to be on?" he asked, hoping Candy had that information and they didn't have to check every one.

He could already hear the sounds of screaming in the distance, but the way it echoed around the large, open, concrete structure of the car park meant that he couldn't pinpoint where it was coming from. He was surprised that the car park wasn't flooded with people all trying to flee whatever was happening inside or get back to their cars to escape and feel safer while they did so.

"It's up beside the food court," Candy said.

"That's the top floor," David acknowledged, running for the set of lifts.

"We'd be safer and quicker with the stairs."

"My legs are still trembling from your rally driver impressions. I'll definitely be quicker in the lift and look, the lights aren't moving at all which means they aren't being used. You take the stairs if you want. I'll see you up there."

"Not a chance. If you're taking the lift, then so am I. We're not splitting up."

Their frantic journey here and their sprint to the lift seemed mildly ridiculous as David pressed the button and they waited for few seconds, standing around as if they were simply out for a relaxed shopping trip. It was the same when the lift arrived. The doors slid open and they both dived inside, pressing the button for the very top floor of the shopping centre. They looked at one another awkwardly as the doors closed and the lift began to move.

"I know this was the sensible option to conserve energy and it will get us there much quicker than the six flights of stairs we'd need to run up, but I think I'll be doing the stairs next time regardless. I feel silly just standing here."

"Me too," Candy agreed.

"Tell me what you know."

"Not much, it was too big an emergency. The gate is across from the food court, probably the worst place it could be in terms of civilian onlookers and possible casualties. That's about it, all I know, except that it's big—really big."

"So why isn't the car park filled with people running for their lives, and the exits gridlocked with cars trying to escape? And why is no one using the lifts? I'd have thought every possible option to get away would have been jam packed."

"I don't know," Candy replied just as the lift gave a soft ping. "But I guess we're about to find out because we're here."

They glanced at one another as the doors slid open, then looked to see what exactly they'd be facing this time. Whatever it was, it already sounded horrific.

Chapter Sixteen

The sounds of screams, shouts, and sobs had intensified to an almost deafening level.

Before David and Candy could react, two absolute mountains of men blocked their path, steeping in front of the open lift. They were all mile wide chests and shoulders, thick bull necks, and bulging biceps. "Sorry, this floor is closed. Suspected security issue that may cause a danger to public safety. Please make your way back down and exit the shopping centre in a calm manner. A full evacuation may be imminent."

Candy smirked at the vague, lame-sounding story. "What kind of security issue?"

"I'm sorry; I can't disclose any more information than that at this time."

She giggled and slapped one of them playfully on his meaty chest, finding that his rock hard pecs stung her hand a little. She pouted and shook it as she spoke. "Pathetic answer that'll fool no one. Even I could have come up with something more convincing than that. Anyway, we're not shoppers, silly."

The man gave her a vacant look. "No one gets beyond this point."

David assumed that the men were probably muscle for hire acquired by the Realm to help keep the public safe, but assuming that didn't help in knowing how much they knew or didn't know, and what could and couldn't be said to them regarding who they were. He wasn't sure how they were going to gain access to where they were meant to be. He dodged and weaved, trying to get a glimpse beyond them to see if there was anyone around that he recognised, anyone that could tell these two gentlemen to give them access to the floor. He could barely see daylight beyond them, let alone anything else that was going on.

Candy didn't have any such concerns. With a hand placed on one massive chest, she looked the man in the eye and gave him a coquettish smile. "Do I look like I'm going to shop in any of these stores to you, or do I look like I eat any of that junk food? I mean, really? I'm a Watcher and David is my Gatekeeper. Let us through."

It seemed to be the magic words. They snapped to attention and leapt aside. Candy and David exploded out of the lift, aware of how much time had already been wasted.

"I would put out of order signs on the lifts and shut them down," Candy called back. "Your act sucks."

"Wow, it *is* huge," David said, immediately forgetting all about the two security men that were guarding the lift as he spotted the gate for the first time. "I can see the edge of it from here! I know I haven't seen many yet but this is much bigger than I've seen before. It runs right from the specialist cupcake shop all the way down to the art shop at the far end, and it goes right up through the roof. They've always been perfect circles before so that means the circumference…oh my goodness; I don't even want to know what that means for how big the circumference is."

Candy appreciated his trying to give her an idea of the scale of what they were dealing with and understood why that would be the focus of *his* attention, but she was only half listening. People were running around like maniacs, slapping or flapping at their ankles, kicking out their legs, confusion and panic in both their shouts and on their faces. She couldn't see the cause but could guess what they might be experiencing. Teeth marks were appearing on the exposed ankles –most of them drawing blood – and she could see rips and tears appearing in trouser legs as if the material was being savaged by hundreds of tiny teeth. The people must be terrified, especially when they couldn't even see what was attacking them. Her heart went out to them but she also knew there wasn't much she could do. All she could offer was advice to get their legs and feet up to a higher level to see if it helped but they were figuring that out on their own anyway. Her main concern was the danger to David and right now, her senses were humming with it. "It's not safe for you here, not safe at all."

"Seekers?" David asked.

"I don't know," Candy wailed. "Probably, but there is too much confusion and high emotion, it's clouding everything for me. I can't even tell which direction the danger will come from and that's not normal. We should get out of here."

"I have to stay, it doesn't matter how dangerous it is. This gate is going to need an awful lot of us to close it. There are a handful of people gathered in front of it so I assume they're Gatekeepers, but they all look quite young and there's hardly any. I'm going to join them."

David sprinted off and Candy ran with him, knowing he was about to be right in front of the gate and directly in the firing line of whatever was coming through. "What are the monsters?"

"Little…oh, I want to say dogs but I don't even know what they are. They're about the size of a small dog, maybe a Yorkshire terrier, but a whole lot less cute. Their jaws are squarer and the teeth are long and spiky, coming to points. Ugh, a bite from those would really hurt."

"That'll be why everyone's screaming," Candy said with a roll of her eyes.

Her sarcasm was simply her go-to coping mechanism. She wasn't really exasperated by David's stating of the obvious. In fact, she was actually thinking that she was really impressed that he'd ran all this way and spoken to her the entire time and wasn't even the slightest bit out of breath. She took a split second to congratulate herself on how much she'd improved his fitness and stamina in such a short time. It would make the world of difference to every mission and could be the difference between life and death for him, or maybe even for an awful lot of people. Still, the monsters this time didn't sound too bad, even with the nasty bite they could give. She hoped the Gatekeepers that had arrived first hadn't seen anything worse loitering just on the other side of the gate. They didn't seem to be doing anything much at the moment, merely standing around and looking confused.

"Someone give me an update, please," David said as he reached them.

"We don't know anything," a skinny boy said with a shrug. "We've all just got here ourselves and there's no one here to tell us what to do."

Candy and David glanced at one another. As far as David was concerned, no Gatekeeper should need to be given specific instructions when faced with an emergency situation like this; they should know instinctively what to do. He decided he'd better take charge. "Where are your Watchers?"

"Over there," a girl said, pointing to where a huddle of people stood not too far away.

"Candy, go and join them and see if they're sensing the danger too. Maybe as a joint group you can figure out what it is and neutralise it."

She nodded and jogged across to them.

David addressed the other Gatekeepers, "We need to get these little critters back through the gate. Concentrate your mind on them, imagine them being dragged all the way across the mall and right back through the opening of the gate."

"Should we imagine pulling them by the tail or the ears? Both seem a bit cruel," one said.

"It doesn't matter because we're not *really* pulling them physically, only with our minds, and I don't think we have to make it that specific. Just imagine them flying back in this direction, right past us and back through to their own world."

The girl looked a little puzzled and David wondered if any of these four Gatekeepers understood what he was saying or if it sounded like he was speaking a foreign language to them. It didn't matter. He was going to get on with his job, even if the others were simply going to stand around and gawk at him.

He turned to face the food court, his back to the gate. He noticed that quite a lot of Hoogle had turned up while he'd been occupied, but he didn't pay them much heed. As long as he didn't let them wander into his thoughts, he wouldn't include any of them as he tried to send the other creatures back through their gate. They seemed to be having fun chasing the dog-type beasts around and reaching out to swipe at them before leaping away up onto chairs and tables as the things turned round to snap at them. If it weren't for all the hurt and scared people, he might almost find the scene funny. Knowing he had no option but to spoil the Hoogle's game as soon as possible, he focused his mind on the critters. He could feel the pull he was exerting on them but there were so many it wasn't nearly enough. He needed to combine the strength and focus of all the Gatekeepers as he'd done the last time. He felt around with his mind, trying to locate the vibrations of the others. All he found were singular strands going to one creature at a time, and they were completely locked down to him. These four had no real idea how to use their powers yet, or how to open them up to the full capacity. David realised he would need to attempt a crash course or they were never going to get this situation under control, not on their own.

While David was trying to find a way to link the Gatekeepers and maximise their ability, Candy was quizzing the other Watchers. She was still extremely on edge over the danger she could feel, and yet, it still wasn't revealing itself clearly to her.

"Can any of you guys feel something…off?" Candy asked the Watchers.

"There's an open gate in a place full of civilians, of course, something's off," a balding man in his mid-forties snapped at her.

"Wow, keep your hair on, granddad. That wasn't what I meant. I'm not dumb enough to have missed that part."

"Could have fooled me."

Now that was just mean, Candy thought, but decided to let it go. Bickering amongst themselves wouldn't get them anywhere. "What I meant was can anyone else feel Seekers around?"

"I don't know how we're supposed to be able to tell anything in this melee," a boy not much older than herself answered. "Besides, I can't sense Seekers until they're practically on top of me. Are you feeling something bad?"

"Yeah, something more than just a Seeker or two, but I can't put my finger on it or get a fix on it," Candy said peering around. "Keep your eyes peeled and stay alert."

She assessed the situation several times over, scanning the entire floor as far as she could see and always keeping half an eye on David as she did so. Practically nothing changed between sweeps. People and shop staff alike were in a state of utter panic, being attacked by unseen teeth or claws. Most of them were now standing on chairs or tables, hugging one another, some crying. The goons were still guarding the various stairs and lifts, which explained why the chaos hadn't spread and the car park wasn't gridlocked with people trying to get out as they were preventing anyone from leaving as well as new people coming up.

She tensed as a group of men charged up one of the staircases and looked around with keen, sharp eyes. She was back by David's side in a flash as they pointed past the goons in the direction of the Gatekeepers, shoving them aside. Candy soon breathed a sigh of relief when she realised they were from the Realm, summoned here to take control of the situation and arrived at last. They attempted to talk to the Gatekeepers but none of them answered, all of them lost in another world where their minds were tentatively learning to reach out to one another and link, gently guided by David. Candy updated them on what she could; telling them what little David had told her about both the gate and the creatures. "I also get the feeling there are Seekers here," she added. "But I can't see them yet."

"Well, that's your department so you can worry about them. We're here to coordinate the Gatekeepers. I don't know why there are so few of them," he said, his eyebrows beetling together in a frown. "There were much more than this summoned and all of the first responders should have been here by now."

Candy couldn't help him with that any more than he could help her with her Seeker issue so she simply shrugged. It looked like she was on her own to deal with her concern. She encouraged the handful of other Watchers to form a line of defence, starting at one end of the Gatekeepers and spreading out in front of them as best as they could with so few of them. Each one of them had to watch all directions, which wasn't ideal, but it was the best they could do in the circumstances.

With the Watchers blind and the Gatekeepers with their backs to the gate, what happened next took everyone by surprise.

Suddenly, three of the Gatekeepers, including David, were sent flying through the air, as were two Watchers that were standing in front of them. Before anyone could get their bearings, the barrier that separated the food court was flattened, then chairs and tables and the people standing on them were being scattered, flung, or even squashed flat in some cases. It looked as if something massive had come charging through the gate. Candy tore her eyes away from the devastation and dashed back to David's side, helping him to his feet. "Are you okay?"

"Yes, just a little taken aback and a touch winded. Geez, will you look at that thing!" David's eyes were wide, his face a horrid shade of grey-green. "Even the Hoogle have scarpered out of its way."

"Remember you said I wouldn't want to know," Candy replied, looking a little sick herself purely from the carnage she could see and David's reaction. "Can you handle it?"

"I could really do with a lot more Gatekeepers but we have to try," he replied. "Everyone, minds off the little things for now and focus on that giant beast!"

"Look out everyone, there's another one!"

With so few Gatekeepers and so many creatures, David felt a wave of despair wash over him. He absolutely refused to give in to it. If he was going to fail and go down, he would do it fighting tooth and nail. He put everything he had into attempting to pull the ginormous creature back to the gate before it rampaged any further through the food court. His mind wouldn't even settle on a description for it; it was simply too frightening for it to cope with. At least they had the adults from the Realm to encourage them and help coordinate them now.

Candy went to check on the Watchers that had been knocked over, knowing she would need them all capable of fighting. She still felt the hum of danger in the air and felt it prickle at the nape of her neck. Luckily, none of the Watchers seemed to be seriously injured. "Where do you think all the others are? There should be much more."

"I was thinking the same thing," one of them answered her.

At that exact moment, a sound very much like an air horn went off, causing everyone to wince and many to slap their hands over their ears to minimise the invasive and deafening sound. As muscle-bound men dressed in black suddenly left their posts and charged forward with malicious grins on their faces, Candy realised with absolute horror what it was she'd been missing all along. "It's the security!" she screamed to the others in warning. "They aren't here with the Realm at all. They must be working for the Seekers!"

The men in black t-shirts and black combats were all converging as they ran, heading directly for the Gatekeepers.

"Not on my watch," Candy said and gave a battle cry as she leapt in front of a small cluster of them, immediately kicking and punching, hands and feet flying in all directions.

These men were hired muscle only, all brute force and no particular finesse. Her moves were highly effective against them. She guessed that they'd always been able to rely on their appearance for intimidation and weren't really used to actually having to fight. Encouraged by Candy's success and their confidence inspired by the lack of training or any real knowledge displayed by the security men, the others readily joined in the fight against them.

"Take that, meathead!" Candy yelled gleefully as she scissor kicked one, catching him under his chin.

She shot out a hand to catch another on the neck just below the ear, dropping him instantly to the ground.

"Oh no, you don't!"

She'd caught another two trying to sneak past the Watchers and get to the Gatekeepers, their hungry eyes set on David specifically. That was when Candy had her suspicions that he was the main target here today. "Over my dead body."

She grabbed the two of them by the hair and slammed their heads together. It was almost a cartoon move but the clash of the two solid skulls most definitely served to put them off balance and she took advantage, fighting street dirty with a kidney punch to one and a toe kick to the back of the knee for the other. It was going well up until the point that the Seekers, seeing their goons being outfought by only a handful of Watchers, decided to step in themselves. They seemed to come out of the woodwork, appearing from shops, corridors, staff only areas, from behind counters, and out from among the civilians at the food court tables.

"There's too many of them," the older Watcher with the bald head said. "They're always skilled fighters. We can't possibly keep them all at bay. Our Gatekeepers are done for."

"They are if you're giving up just like that," Candyretorted. "If you don't want to fight, then fine, just go, get out of my way. Just remember that if anything happens to me I was fighting for the lives of all the Gatekeepers, yours included."

The man took a brief second to look ashamed, but then there was no time as they were overrun by

Seekers. Side by side, they fought for all they were worth, even though they knew it was futile. There was no way the five of them could beat this many Seekers and their hired helpers.

CHAPTER SEVENTEEN

David could see that the Watchers were struggling, but he had his own fight on his hands. Even though these four inexperienced and unconfident Gatekeepers were finally getting the hang of entwining their focus together and joining their power, all of them were struggling to even so much as contain the massive beast, let alone pull it back through the gate. The smaller creatures that had overtaken the mall earlier were running riot again, all the focus taken from them and now being directed towards the new and much worse threat. Even if the thing turned out to be vegan, it was still a bad tempered brute that liked to smash and crush. They'd managed to restrain it of sorts but their control was slipping. In fact, they were losing control of this entire situation. The adults from the Realm were calling out instructions and encouragement, but they couldn't see what David could see and had no idea how much it was taking out of him just to hold the thing.

"We need more! Where are they?" one of the adults from the Realm asked.

"I don't know," one of the men said. "They should have been here by now."

"Can't you make some calls or something?"

"It should already be organised."

"Well, obviously it isn't, or something's gone wrong," David explained, trying to sound gentle, even though he was having to yell over all the noise. "Either way, you're going to need to tell someone to organise a lot more Gatekeepers, no matter how long it's going to take for them to get here. We'll just have to try and hold things until they do."

He wasn't quite sure exactly *how* he was going to hold things until that time; he just knew he had to find a way.

For Candy and the other Watchers, things were equally dire. They'd dispersed of the fake security guards easily enough and they were all down with injuries that would ensure they wouldn't get up again during this particular fight. But dealing with them had used up the Watchers' energy and had distracted them from some of the Seekers' initial attacks. The Watchers all carried some minor injuries, or several of them. They were struggling to keep the Seekers from reaching the Gatekeepers, gradually being pushed aside or backwards to where they couldn't protect them, being manoeuvred too far away from them.

Candy glanced to her left, seeing the younger Watcher that she'd conversed with earlier put up a brave fight, battling to gain back some ground against the two Seekers that were trying to push him back towards the gate. She mentally cheered him on, willing him to succeed. The next moment, she was letting out an anguished scream.

"No!"

One of the Seekers had pulled a knife, not using it for intimidation nor threat, not hesitating for a second before thrusting it hard between the Watcher's ribs and plunging it deep towards his heart. Crimson exploded and he dropped to the ground, his eyebrows raised, his mouth open in an 'o' of surprise. His hands went up to clutch the wound that remained behind as the Seeker pulled the knife free with an evil grin. He turned towards another Watcher.

Candy wanted nothing more than to take down the one with the knife and make sure it couldn't be used on any of the others, but the Seekers had figured out that Candy was their greatest adversary and the biggest threat. They were ganging up on her, converging together in a group and advancing on her. She'd fought hard, she'd fought bravely, but she knew her time was almost up.

She didn't give up but the sheer number of them ensured they managed to steer her where they wanted her to go. Now she was backed into a corner up against a wall, nowhere to run, nowhere to hide, no way to get through them to stop any more killing, and no way to get to David's side to protect him. She was battered and bruised all over, hurt in various places, exhausted. She couldn't go on any longer. In her head, she said a silent and heartbroken goodbye, wishing David well, and hoping that he would survive this and find a new, better Watcher, one that would never let him down. Over the shoulders of the Seekers that had gathered around her, she saw another Watcher being grabbed and unceremoniously tossed through the gate, left to the fate of whatever monsters and nightmares lay beyond. She had no time to dwell on it or give in to the tears that welled for the lives already lost here today. The Seekers were still advancing.

They were now upon her, punching her in the face, about her head and neck, in the stomach, in the back, over and over. She tried to block and parry but the hits were coming from too many different directions. It was hopeless. She closed her eyes, felt her hair being grasped and used to pull her to the ground where angry feet began to lay into her from all sides. She curled up into a ball and waited for the end, hoping she would at least pass out before it happened.

Suddenly, it all stopped.

Am I dead? No, I can't be, she thought. *I still ache absolutely everywhere and I can still hear all the terrible sounds.* Tentatively, she opened one eye. What she saw made no sense to her. The Seekers were acting as if they were being attacked, all trying to reach for something that seemed to be on their backs, trying to shield their eyes from something that was trying to scratch at them from behind. This action was accompanied by them leaping or hopping around, occasionally slapping at their ankles as if something had them there too. She was relieved but didn't know what was happening, so she couldn't guess how long this reprieve might last. Had something else come through the gate and joined the ankle biters? She needed to get up or she would be next on their menu.

She scrambled to her feet, pain shooting through every part of her body as she did so. Most of the Seekers seemed occupied, the Watchers standing bemused as they saw them being attacked by an invisible enemy. She had to know what was going on. The information could be essential. As fast as she could, she limped and hobbled her way over to David, clutching at her ribs as she went, reluctant to interrupt him but having no choice.

"David," she panted when she reached him, the pain having stolen her breath. "Sorry, but what's happening with the Seekers?"

David looked over to where she pointed and even under such awful circumstances managed a grin. "It's the Hoogle! They're jumping on their backs and putting their hands over their eyes, and seemed to have persuaded their little doggy playmates to go on the attack and target only them. Either that or the little dog things are just trying to get at the Hoogle, hence, why they're only going for people with Hoogle on their backs. I can't tell but it's obviously providing a distraction."

"How long will they be able to hold them? We're in big trouble here."

"Tell me about it. I don't think we're going to be able to hold out much longer either. It doesn't look like the Hoogle will be able to help for long. The Seekers are already figuring out how to pull them off by their tails or to slam them against walls. They're doing their best but they don't seem to be cut out for fighting."

Candy nodded, wanting to say so much but knowing it wasn't the time, might never be the time. David was busy and she'd distracted him for too long already. Now that she knew what was happening to the Seekers, she could re-join the battle and try to help the Hoogle keep them at bay for just that little bit longer, to buy David maybe a few more minutes at least.

"Hang on, Hoogle, I'm coming to help!"

She leapt back in; giving what she thought would be one last battle cry.

Candy and David weren't aware, but even the representatives of the Realm had come to terms with this being the end of everything as they knew it. There was no possible way this could be contained and controlled. It was out of hand. Every Gatekeeper and Watcher here were going to die at the hands of the Seekers, and probably the Seekers and civilians would die at the hands of whatever came through the gate. There was simply no way to win.

Just as hope had all about died in everyone, hordes of people exploded onto the top floor of the shopping mall, bursting from every lift, piling up every set of stairs. Gatekeepers of all ages finally arrived and rushed over to where David and the other youngsters were trying to keep things together.

"Oh, you have got to be kidding me," a man in his late thirties said. "A Kongadiplothaurus? I haven't seen one of those in years. Oh, wow, you managed to create a power link between you. Nice job, kiddo, I'm impressed! We'll all just tap into that and add to it."

David felt the sudden jolt of power as all the new arrivals added their considerable combined ability to his own. Now they would finally begin to make some headway with this! They began with the gigantic creature, the Konga-whatever-he'd-called-it thingy, doing just as much damage to the fixtures and fittings as their mind power dragged it back across the centre as it had done when it had rampaged across it in the first place. Soon, they were letting out a massive cheer as they threw it back through the gate.

"Yes!" David yelled, pumping the air with his fist and jumping on the spot. "Right, ten of you, or more if need be, on gate duty to make sure that one stays there. Another ten hold the perimeter of the gate. We don't want anything else coming through. I'm worried about the part of it we can't see, too. We need a group up on the roof if possible."

"I'll organise that," one of the Realm's agents said, much more positive and stepping up now that he had people to work with. He could spare them up there now that there was plenty to go around.

Leaving him to organise that part, David turned back to the very large group of Gatekeepers. "We need to deal with everything else. The Hoogle didn't come through this gate so leave them be, but let's get those doggy things home, even if they are attacking the Seekers, the new Watchers can take care of them now. We need to get this gate shut down."

With all of them working together and the massive infusion of new energy, the job was soon done. The new Watchers, with a little help from the mischievous Hoogle, soon had the Seekers subdued, restrained, and ready to be dealt with by the clean-up crew.

"All clear from the roof," a Realm representative called out after a conversation on a walkie-talkie.

"That's the go ahead to close this thing," David said gratefully.

The Gatekeepers took great pleasure in doing just that and soon they were all high-fiving and congratulating one another. The man who'd spoken to David earlier made a point of tracking him down to speak to him again. "It looks like you did a fabulous job of coordinating everything and I can't believe that there aren't any fatalities here today caused by what came through the gate. A Kongadiplothaurus is one of the most dangerous things I've ever encountered and up there on the list of top twenty in the Realm's archives. It's also one of the strongest, so I'm amazed that a small group of newbies even managed to hold it relatively still. Well done."

"Thanks a lot," David replied the man, "but I don't think I could have done it much longer, not if you guys hadn't arrived. What kept you anyway?"

The guy shook his head, a look of disgust on his face. "A whole bunch of fake security shutting the place down. Every route up here was blocked by them. They kept telling us it wasn't safe for us to go up yet, making out that we were the first on the scene. We had no idea you guys were up here. They stalled us forever before we figured out something wasn't right about them, and then we had to fight our way through when we did. Sorry we took so long."

"Not your fault. My Watcher said there was something off here right from the start. Speaking of which, I really need to go and make sure she's okay. She wasn't looking too good last time I saw her. Oh, hey, before I go, did you see what the Hoogle were up to?"

"Yeah, they seemed to go a little crazy. Maybe all the energy sent them into a frenzy."

"That's what you think? Did you notice that it was only the Seekers that they were jumping on?"

The Gatekeeper's eyebrows shot up. "I didn't notice at the time but now that you mention it, yeah, yeah, I think you're right. Still must be a coincidence. The little devils don't have that kind of reasoning power and wouldn't have any reason to help us even if they did."

He wandered off, shaking his head. David mentally filed away the fact that the man had obviously never seen the Hoogle acting that way previously. He would need to give that some serious thought later. In the meantime, he really did need to find Candy. He was incredibly worried about her.

He eventually located her with the officials from the Realm and came upon them as Candy was in the middle of a speech that was growing a touch heated.

"…not wasting time applying to anyone for permission or anything else. You say you don't have the authority to authorise this and I say I don't care, *I'm* authorising it! We have hundreds of civilians here who've witnessed things they can't explain, and *not* witnessed things that are even harder to explain. They're going to be telling everyone they know, selling stories to the tabloids, talking to therapists, whatever. The point is they're going to be doing an awful lot of talking, and that'll attract far too much attention. Also, if we don't do this, these people will be traumatised for the rest of their lives and I won't have it. If the Realm has a problem with that then they can come see me later."

Leaving the officials stunned and chastised, Candy turned on her heel and gathered the Watchers together. She quickly coordinated them all to work on large groups of anyone not involved in their world, altering their memories within mere moments. She had struggled to come up with a story, being on the top floor of the building made it hard to use something like a natural gas leak or an earthquake. She eventually came up with a rare and unusual, fast breeding species of rodent. She borrowed from various movies, using the plot of a small family of them making their home in a packing crate of foodstuffs to be imported, surviving the journey, then escaping into the mall when the crate had been opened after delivery at one of the more exotic franchises in the food court. She'd been pleased enough with the story and the other Watchers had shrugged and agreed it sounded okay. At least it could explain all the unusual bite marks that couldn't be hidden and would need to be treated.

Reassured that she was okay, David watched Candy work. It was a fascinating and rapid process, and it was amazing to think that the secrets of the Realm would stay safe because of it.

She'd just finished with her last group and David had begun to walk towards her when a bald-headed man sidled up, cutting David off in his path. "I just wanted to come and say thank you," he said to Candy.

"Thank you for what?" Candy asked with a puzzled smile.

"The way you fought and refused to give up. I think if it weren't for you, the fake security guards would have overpowered us before we realised what was happening, and I know for a fact that if it weren't for you, we would have all given in when we were so close to being overwhelmed by the Seekers. We and our Gatekeepers would have been dead by now."

"Oh, don't talk nonsense," Candy said with a giggle and flap of her hand. "You wouldn't have let that happen no matter what, and I didn't do that much anyway."

The man looked disbelieving at first but as he gazed at Candy's vacant smile, David could see that he was beginning to doubt his own conviction in the heroic and the essential role she'd played. He nodded, unsure of himself now, and wandered off.

David strolled over. "You might have been able to fool him but you don't fool me. You were quite the hero today and I don't doubt for a second that every word he said was true. You saved hundreds of lives here today."

"I didn't do it without an awful lot of help. Everyone played a massive part in there being only injuries and no deaths, even the Hoogle. What was that all about, though?""I don't know, but I think we'll be talking about it in great detail in a private later, right?"

"Absolutely, and you'll have to thank the little guys for me since I can't even see them to give them as much as a nod."

"I'll do just that."

"Right then, we're done here. The clean-up crew will take care of everything else and we should go before there are police and paramedics everywhere. Are you able to take the stairs this time?"

"I'm fine for the stairs but I'm not so sure you are," David said, looking at the way she was holding her side and keeping all her weight mostly on one leg. "How badly are you hurt?"

"I'm perfectly fine," she said brightly.

David knew it was bravado on her part and although she would heal quickly, she really could do with a good, long rest right now. The sooner they got home the better. The problem was that there was a max exodus of Gatekeepers and their Watchers leaving right now, as well as operatives from the Realm carting off the Seekers and fake security guards. He didn't want to take Candy into the crush when she was already in pain, but he could hear a cacophony of sirens in the distance. The police would be here soon and everyone would be kept for questioning for hours on end. David suggested, "Do you think you could make it down two flights of stairs so we're down a level? That way we'll just look like innocent shoppers who weren't involved in this and can wait until the gridlock has cleared before we try to leave."

"Of course, I can."

Squaring her shoulders, Candy made her way to the stairs where she battled her way to the side railing and leaned on it heavily all the way down, trying to avoid her painful ribs, stomach, and kidney area being bumped and jostled by the crowds. Once down, David took her arm and put it round his shoulders, leading her to a quiet bench on the far side of the shopping centre, away from the main hustle and bustle. She lowered herself down gently.

"Whew, I made it," she said.

"Is it really bad?"

"Not so much, and you know how quickly I heal. I'll likely be on the mend before we even move from here. I just need a minute or two, that's all."

David let it go, not wanting to push her if she didn't want to admit to anything more. "That was the biggest gate I've ever seen. I wonder how big they can actually get."

"That sort of thing is probably on record at the Realm. They might have their own libraries that you can visit or study material that you can borrow. That would be right up your street."

"It would," David agreed with a grin. "I'll have to look into that. I was worried about the part of the gate we couldn't see today. I didn't have any idea how high it went and the shopping centre isn't that far away from the airport. What if it extended up into flight paths? Do you think a plane could fly right into a gate and not even realise?"

"I guess that could happen."

"That maybe explains a lot of the disappearances of planes and ships and things throughout history!" David exclaimed, his eyes shining with excitement. "That could be the answer to the Bermuda Triangle and everything; they're maybe all gates."

"Maybe they are," Candy replied.

She'd heard of the Bermuda Triangle before, so she knew what he was getting at. It did make her wonder how many times that kind of thing happened. If it hadn't happened here today, then they'd probably been lucky. In fact, they'd been lucky in lots of different ways today. "That was a bad one."

"It was. I can't believe how wrong everything seemed to go. It looked like the Seekers somehow knew in advance that the gate was going to open and had all those people in place."

Candy shuddered. "Maybe they just had everyone on standby and acted really quickly when they got the word. We can hope so anyway. I'd hate to think that the bad guys might have someone on the inside. Anyway, that would be for the Realm to worry about. We just have to think about our part. It nearly ended in disaster."

"We nearly lost control of that gate," David agreed. "But I'm not sure we could have done anything differently. There weren't enough Gatekeepers and the ones that were there didn't have enough experience. It was also the first time I've seen two types of creatures come through one gate, the first time we've had Seekers attacking us while dealing with a gate, and the first time we've arrived before anyone from the Realm was there to coordinate things. I think everything just combined to create a catastrophe, but it could have been so much worse. I might be better prepared for all those things in future."

Candy nodded, her expression sad. "We lost two good Watchers today, at least two that I saw. It might have been more."

"I know, and I'm sorry. The only consolation is that an awful lot of Seekers were captured today. I think the fallen Watchers would be proud and honoured to have taken part in such a monumental battle that had such a positive overall outcome. I'm sure they wouldn't hesitate to do it again, even with hindsight."

"You're right, they wouldn't."

"What frightened me the most was that I might have lost you."

Candy looked up at him and they made eye contact for a brief second. "You almost did, and it would have been a definite if it hadn't been for your little friends. Was that just a lucky coincidence, them being in the right place at the right time? Just them getting up to their usual mischief?"

"I really can't say and this could be wishful thinking, but it did look as if they were deliberately protecting you."

"According to everything your Grandfather said, that would be impossible. He thinks they aren't smart enough for that kind of thing."

"So he says. I'm going to keep an open mind about that one."

Candy felt a sudden vibration in her pocket. "Oh, that's my phone."

Digging it out and answering, she grimaced then did an awful lot of nodding and saying yes, opening her mouth to speak on several occasions but getting no further than that single word if she got any in at all. She finally hung up, still not getting a word in edgeways. "That was your mum, freaking out because she heard about an unknown species of rodent overtaking the mall on the radio. She figured it had to be a gate and that we'd be here. I guess we should go. She isn't going to be happy until she sees for herself that you're fine. I've told her we're on our way home now."

David looked around. "Everything seems to have quietened down now anyway and the centre doesn't seem very busy."

"Is it any wonder if the rat story is out? Would you hang around a building overrun by vermin?"

"Um…no, you're right. Let's go."

They made their way to the closest set of lifts that would take them back down to the level of the car park where Candy had left her car. It was a lesser used set tucked away in this quiet corner, which meant one arrived quickly and was empty when it did. They were soon stepping out of the brightly lit lift and into the gloom of the car park, low ceilings and muted lighting adding to the dingy look and feel of the concrete structure. Candy was looking forward to getting out of here. She hurt all over and wanted nothing more than a long soak in a bath full of bubbles surrounded by scented candles. She tried to focus on that pleasant thought. Somehow, today, this place was giving her the creeps. Every footfall was echoing back at them from a million directions, sounding eerie and unfamiliar. It was unusually silent and deserted; too many empty spaces between cars for the time of day. She was so glad when she reached her own little car that she let out a relieved giggle. She was making her way round to the driver's side when she saw something reflected in the rear window she was passing that turned her blood to ice.

The glimmer of light reflecting off metal from the side of a pillar in the orangey fluorescence was enough to tell her everything she needed to know. Someone was lurking, someone intent on doing maximum harm.

In spite of her pain, no matter how much everything already hurt, she turned, time standing still, hoping against hope that she was in time as she saw the flash go off, heard the gunshot that was almost deafening in this silent, echoing place, and leapt, flying through the air, her body extended as much as possible to make herself the biggest shield that she could.

She felt something ram into her, the force shocking, her body, caught in mid-air, being slammed back against David and the two of them tumbled to the ground. She shoved at him with weak hands, silently telling him to get underneath the car. Everything was crimson as she fumbled for her phone, feeling fuzzy and sleepy, cold and shivery. She found it, pulled it out, tossed it weakly towards David. "Run, hide, call your parents," she managed, her words sounding slurred even to her own ears as lifeblood pumped from her body onto the cold, grey concrete beneath her.

CHAPTER EIGHTEEN

"She's my stepmother."

The paramedic looked at David then dubiously back at the unconscious Candy. David flushed, aware that he'd just told an adult a blatant falsehood, or at the very least greatly exaggerated the truth. He'd done it to get his own way too, not even to protect Realm secrets or anything justifiable to anyone but himself. He felt bad about it but knew it had to be done. He needed to be with Candy. He would never forgive himself if the worst happened and he hadn't been by her side. Tears welled up his eyes at the very thought.

The paramedic shrugged, not having any way to either verify or disprove David's story without further investigation. There simply wasn't the time. His patient was losing a lot of blood and she needed to be in the hospital, preferably in emergency surgery as soon as possible. He wasn't going to stand around and question a boy about a family relationship. "Get in."

David leapt into the back of the ambulance where Candy was already strapped to the gurney and hooked up to a variety of monitors with serious sounding bleeps and flashing lights. From her nose to her fingertips, tubes and lines protruded from her and were attached to something else. It all looked terrifying to David but none of them frightened him as much as the awful colour of grey Candy's face had gone, or the fact that her normally vibrant eyes were closed, not even fluttering beneath the eyelids. She was so still, so quiet. It just wasn't Candy.

The engine started up and David's ears were assaulted by the wail of the siren as the ambulance began to move. He wanted to hold Candy's hand in the hope that she would know he was there with her but he didn't dare, scared that he would interfere with some of the medical equipment that was perhaps keeping her alive. The paramedic in the back of the ambulance completely ignored him, intent on watching the data being produced by his machines. David knew he should be glad that he was being so attentive to his patient but couldn't help wishing that the guy would speak, explain some of the wires or displays; give him a progress report…something…anything.

However, he said nothing and all David could do was stare at Candy, listen to the beeping machines and the wailing sirens, and hope for the best while fearing the worst.

He couldn't quite believe this was happening. They'd just come through their biggest challenge yet together; had both just survived an incredibly dangerous situation where they'd both doubted they were going to get out of alive. The peril had been all over, the risk neutralised, and the Realm had all the tidying up under control. He and Candy had been about to head home, tired yet victorious. Then this. How could it happen?

Someone had been lurking in the shadows, hiding behind the pillars in the gloom of the parking lot by Candy's car, lying in wait for them. David hadn't really known what was going on. He'd heard a sound like an explosion that had practically deafened him, left a ringing in his ears that he couldn't clear no matter how much he shook his head. Then Candy had been crashing into him, shoving him under the car, throwing her phone at him, and there had been blood, so much blood—

"Stop!" David yelled.

The paramedic jumped and glowered at David, not appreciating his strange and unprovoked outburst. "Don't make me regret letting you come along. I'll have my partner stop so I can escort you out if I have to."

"Sorry, sorry," David said, rubbing his hands over his face in an attempt the clear the horrible visions from before and trying to ensure that they didn't overwhelm him again. What had brought him to this moment was quite simple and he should be able to think about it without getting overcome. He wasn't a kid anymore. Candy had been shot; it was as plain as that. Someone had been lying in wait for them. Chances were that it was a Seeker and David was the target. The fact that Candy had taken the bullet was either the Seeker knowing he would have to get the Watcher out of the way first or Candy doing the job she loved to do and doing it well, with no thought for her own wellbeing. He'd tried to tell himself that she wouldn't have wanted it any other way a million times since it'd happened but it being a matter of fact just wasn't helping. Never had he felt only thirteen years old quite so much in his life. Never before had he felt more like a child—small, vulnerable, helpless, and useless. He hadn't had a clue what to do to help Candy, didn't have a clue how to fight someone with a gun or evade someone shooting at him. All he could do was pull her beneath the car with him and call for an ambulance, screaming that someone had been shot and hope for adults to take control. He felt pathetic but this was no time for his self-pity. There was a much bigger issue to worry about, and that was whether Candy was going to survive.

It hadn't taken more than a few moments after his call to the emergency services number for there to be the sound of wailing sirens echoing around the multi-storey car park and then filling it with their haunting sound. David assumed that the shooter had heard him make the call and made his escape, knowing that the place would be crawling with police within moments. At least, that's how he imagined it. It would definitely be what happened in a TV drama or film. He had no real way of knowing for certain but obviously, the mention of a gun had brought the type of response he'd hoped for and police *were* crawling all over the place within moments. They'd known what to do for Candy until the ambulance had arrived. David was thankful for the arrival of responsible adults to take charge and the speed at which they'd come.

He'd seen the wound for the first time as they'd pulled Candy out to assess her condition, an action that was accompanied by lots of sucked in breaths and shaking of heads. The police had bandied around words like slow and suffer alongside the term gut shot. He didn't like the sound of any of that at all. The entire floor of the car park was in chaos as some officers searched for the shooter, some yelled questions at him, while others tried to give Candy lifesaving emergency treatment, but what David didn't like most of all was the amount of blood. He'd never seen so much for real before. It was only later when a paramedic wrapped a blanket around him and he looked down to grasp it in front of him that he realised he was covered in it too, that Candy had bled profusely on him when he'd pulled her beneath the car and placed her head on his lap while he made the call, then held her in his arms afterwards to keep her warm as she'd shivered there uncontrollably.

A million questions had been fired at David once Candy was being treated by the paramedics but he couldn't tell them very much. He hadn't really seen anything and it had all happened so quickly. They'd wanted to take him down to the station immediately but he'd kicked up such a fuss about not leaving Candy that they'd backed off and allowed him to stay close by her as she was worked on frantically and loaded into the back of the vehicle. Now they were hurtling towards the hospital, hoping to save her life.

On arrival at the emergency bay, four police officers were waiting for them. Two accompanied Candy as her gurney was pushed straight through to the operating theatres, the hospital alerted to her imminent arrival and critical condition. The other two officers remained with David as he stood at the swing doors on tiptoe, peering through the circular windows until she was completely out of sight. When he finally turned away from the doors, they escorted him silently to the waiting room and sat down either side of him.

"Can we call anyone for you?"

"I suppose my mother needs to know what's happening. We spoke to her not long beforehand and Candy told her we were heading home. She was expecting us, probably getting really worried by now."

"Give me the number and I'll call for you."

David shook his head. "I should do it. It'll sound an awful lot more frightening coming from you than it would from me. The minute you say you're a police officer, she'll be having kittens and thinking the worst before you even have a chance to explain anything else."

David wasn't sure if mobile phones were allowed in the waiting room so he rose to head outside. The fact that the officers followed him made him uncomfortable. Was he under suspicion of something? He ignored them until he'd stepped outside. But he finally asked them, "Can I have some privacy please?"

They glanced at one another and David caught the almost imperceptible nod that the elder gave to the younger. The younger of the two turned to David. "Okay, but not too far, though. We need to keep you in sight. You haven't been formally interviewed yet but we'd need a responsible adult with you for that anyway. Parents are best if they're available and willing."

"Mine will be," David replied.

He had absolutely no doubt that his parents would be here in a heartbeat, for Candy and for him, and that his mother would take control over this situation. He needed to tell her as much as possible without sending her into an absolute panic. She needed to be prepared with her story so she didn't say anything about the Realm or disclose anything she shouldn't. He sighed. It wasn't going to be the easiest of calls.

A few minutes later, he was holding the phone away from his ear, still able to hear his mum clearly at the other end. He'd told her what had happened in the car park and she was already over the first wave of horror and shock, had been through the phase of offering sympathy and comfort and now, assured that David was unharmed, was currently going ballistic, furious that anyone or anything that wasn't a mindless creature from another world would dare to try and harm her son. He supposed it was a natural enough reaction and waited patiently while she worked through it. Finally, she got past it and was ready to move on.

"Right, I'll call your father and we'll both meet you at the hospital. I won't tell him how bad Candy is until after we get there. He won't be any good to anyone if he has an accident on the way. Don't say anything else to the police. They can't formally question you until we're there with you anyway."

"Do you think we should call the Realm to help us with that?"

"I don't think it'll be necessary. We'll call them if we need to but I think it would be a bit premature at this stage. I can't foresee any problems. You were the ones that were shot at when innocently leaving the shopping centre. You haven't done anything wrong, haven't got a clue what it might have been about, and didn't even see anything that could help. Understood?"

"Got it."

"But just don't say anything at all anyway, not a word."

"Yes, Mum," he said, thanking his lucky stars that she couldn't see him rolling his eyes.

"Good, we'll be there soon."

"Thank you, I'll be glad to see you."

"Right." Jill's brisk tone disappeared and her voice softened. "David, how bad is it?"

"Nobody told me anything but it looked really bad, and it seemed pretty urgent. I don't think it's looking too good."

He heard a chocked back sob but when Jill spoke again, she was completely in control. "I'm on my way."

David hung up and wandered back inside. There seemed nothing more for him to do except wait.

***

David's face had been a mask of pity as he'd watched William leap to his feet every time anyone in a white coat or scrubs entered the waiting area, looking toward them with pleading and hopeful eyes. Each time so far, he'd been disappointed, the member of hospital staff looking to talk to someone else about some other patient, or in there for another reason entirely. It hadn't stopped William, though, and this time his efforts were rewarded. The theatre nurse headed straight for them, the two police officers in their party a bit of a giveaway that they were ones waiting for news of the shooting victim.

"Hi, I'm Laura Callaghan, a surgical nurse." She shook hands with Jill and William, only considering David worthy of a quick glance. "I've been in the theatre with the surgeons and Candy since her arrival. I'm pleased to tell you that she's finally out of surgery and has been moved to intensive care."

"Can I see her?" David said, leaping in as soon as the nurse paused to take a breath.

"No visitors yet I'm afraid, but I can give you an indication of our findings and how the surgery went."

"Please do," William said, placing his hands on David's shoulders to let him know he wanted no further interruptions. He needed to hear what the nurse had to say.

"The bullet nicked her liver, causing major trauma to her body and severe blood loss. We have everything under control, the internal bleeding stopped, and she's had a transfusion. All her vital signs are stable at the moment. She's still unconscious but that's a good thing for now, giving her body more chance to focus on healing. She's not out of the woods yet as there's always a chance her body could go into delayed shock and start shutting down. The liver could start bleeding again, or infection could set in, but given the amount of vital organs and major blood vessels in the area, she's actually been a very lucky young woman that there wasn't a lot more damage done. The odds are looking favourable for a full recovery provided there are no secondary complications, but she will need a bit of time and a lot of TLC."

David's expression turned from pained to blessed relief as the fingers that had been digging into his shoulders loosened their grip. He was glad that the strong hands remained there, though, bringing him comfort and perhaps offering some, too. It made him think about everyone that was on his side and how much they would give for him, especially Candy.

"So when can we see her?" William was asking.

"I'm not sure yet. We'll have to wait for the I.C.U. doctors to okay that once they've examined her. It could be a while, and it might be that she sleeps right through the night anyway. Even if she does wake up, she's going to be very groggy from the anaesthetic and the pain relief we'll need to keep her on. She might not even really know who you are. You'd probably be as well going home and coming back tomorrow. You can call last thing and first thing for an update from the nurses' desk if that would make you feel better."

"No, I'm not leaving her," William said. "Not until she wakes up enough to know that I'm here for her."

"Me neither," David agreed.

"Nor me," Jill added.

The nurse gave a small smile. "Fair enough. I would suggest you maybe make sure you all get something to eat and make yourselves comfortable. This could be a long wait. I'll let the intensive care nurses know you're all staying and ask them to come and advise you if there's any change and keep you posted with any updates."

"Thank you, nurse. We appreciate that," Jill said.

The nurse returned Jill's smile and left them to it. Jill turned her attention to William and David. "You heard what she said. Does anyone want to nip to the canteen for something to eat while we know for sure she's sleeping and isn't going to wake up in a hurry?"

"No thanks, love. I really don't have any appetite at all," William replied.

"I couldn't eat a thing either," David added. "I actually feel a little sick."

"That'll likely be the shock hitting you now that you know she's stable and can relax a little. It's a normal reaction and you've done well to hold it together until now. I think what we all need is a nice cup of hot, sweet tea. I'll go and fetch us some from the café. It's bound to be much nicer than anything out of that vending machine."

"That sounds good."

Jill smiled gratefully at William. She knew he probably didn't mean it, but also knew that he understood that she needed to be doing something and feeling as if she were helping. She headed out of the waiting room and along the corridor, back towards where the cafeteria was located, thinking that if they had any pre-packed sandwiches, she might pick some of them up too, just in case either of them changed their minds and felt peckish later on. Maybe some crisps or biscuits too in case they were still hungry or felt the need for some sugar as a boost. She would see what the cafe had to offer and decide then. The thought made her feel much better, made her feel as if she had some control over the outcome.

Chapter Nineteen

It was late, or rather it was early.

It was after one o'clock in the morning. Candy had eventually woken up enough to be cleared for a very short spell of visitors. They'd been allowed to speak to her for only a few moments each, one at a time, and only until the nurses had chased them away saying that they were tiring their patient too much.

David had put on a brave face during his few minutes with her, chatting, talking about how well she'd done, how well the surgery had gone, how she was going to be fine, and talking about how she was his hero yet again for saving his life. He joked with her that taking bullets was possibly beyond the call of duty, even for a Watcher. He'd done everything he could to hide how much seeing her hurt this badly and lying there had affected him emotionally. She looked so small, so thin, so fragile. She was still hooked up to all the frightening machines, monitors for this and drips for that. He'd barely been able to get near her bed for all the equipment and tubes everywhere. She'd responded to him, giving him the ghost of a smile, but it was obviously hard for her to do so, and that even turning her head towards him as he spoke seemed to hurt. Her small face was pinched with pain in spite of the pain relief with which she'd no doubt been heavily medicated. Her lids flickered and drooped as she fought to stay awake to acknowledge him. He'd choked back tears, torn between being by her side and leaving her in peace. He didn't really know what to say or what to do. He wasn't equipped for this type of situation. Once more, he was acutely aware of the fact that he was just a stupid kid that didn't really know anything about life or what to do in bad situations. He'd never been cocky like many of his classmates, but this made him far more aware of all his self-doubts, uncertainties, and failings than ever before. He also didn't have a clue what it would feel like to be shot, but he felt bad enough just being part of the experience and having to witness it happening to someone he cared about. He felt drained, wrung out. His entire body ached, he felt weak, tired, over emotional, as if someone had put him through one of those mangle things he'd seen in one of his history books.

William had insisted on staying, refusing to leave the hospital, even if he wasn't allowed to be in Candy's room to watch over her. He claimed he wanted the nurses to be able to tell her he was there every single time she woke up, even if she would be too groggy to remember. Jill and David both understood.

"I'll stay too," David said, exhausted but not wanting to be seen as doing less than his father.

"I don't think so, young man," Jill said. "You need to come home and get some sleep."

"I want to stay, for Candy and to keep Dad company."

Jill was adamant. There was no way she was going to let him remain on an all-night vigil in the waiting room. She could see that he was overtired and close to breaking point. She didn't blame him for that at all, of course. She hadn't even heard about what had happened with the breach in the shopping centre, but as bad as it had or hadn't been, that and what had happened right afterwards would be too much for just about anyone, let alone a thirteen year old boy. She'd actually had something she needed to tell him, but now, she wasn't sure if she should. It was really important, but she wasn't certain if he could handle it right now. Probably best to wait until morning.

With that decision made, she enforced her other. "No, and that's final. You've been through too much today already. You're coming home with me."

"Listen to your mother. I appreciate you wanting to stay and so will Candy when she hears about it, but I'll be fine, son. Everything will be okay, you'll see. You should go."

"But I don't want to. I want to know what's happening."

"I promise I'll call the hospital once we get home for an update and I'll call back again at the break of dawn," Jill said to David. "I'll bring you right back here first thing in the morning provided you manage to eat a little breakfast, but please, David, don't make a fuss right now. You're coming home with me."

He'd been in a sulk but he'd come with her. She'd been grateful, not knowing if she was up for a major fight either. This had all their nerves frayed and they were bound to be testy, fractious, and over sensitive with being so tired. She knew that even at home, David might not get a lot of sleep, but perhaps if he let her make him a cup of cocoa and tuck him in, he might doze off. These were the thoughts that were running through her head as she drove out of the city towards suburbia, looking forward to getting home.

"She is going to be okay, isn't she?" David asked.

The question from the passenger seat almost made her jump. It was the first time David had spoken since they'd left the hospital and she'd been totally lost in her own thoughts. She pulled herself together enough to answer. "She's in the best possible place getting the best possible care. The doctors and nurses think the prognosis is good and so do I."

David wasn't sure if that had been what he wanted to hear. He didn't want a rehash of the nurse speak; he wanted his mum to tell him everything was going to be okay, he wanted comfort and promises, he wanted her to make it all right. He'd known for a few years now that his parents didn't have those magical abilities that he'd believed they'd did when he was small, but he would have given anything to believe in them again just for one more night. Instead, he tried to look at things from a grown up perspective, or maybe a *Gatekeeper* perspective. "Will she be safe there, do you think? I mean, will there be any Seekers trying to finish the job?"

Jill sighed and pointedly refused to glance in David's direction, keeping her eyes firmly on the road. "Do you know more about this than you've had the chance to tell me?"

"No, not really."

"So it is true that you didn't see anything and don't know who attacked you, just like you told the police?"

"Yes, that's true, but I figured a Seeker was a fair assumption. It is, isn't it?"

"Yes, it is."

"You don't sound so sure. What's wrong?"

"Nothing," Jill said, a little too brightly. "I'm sure Candy is safe. A Seeker taking her out would only do so to get to you. Right now, she's not in anyone's way so there would be no need…oh, heavens above. That really didn't come out the way I meant it too, I'm sorry. I'm tired and worried about you both; just ignore me."

"No, you're right, and you shouldn't sugar coat things or baby me. If a Seeker was trying to get to me then this is a perfect chance, and why waste time permanently removing an out of action Watcher who'd just be replaced anyway when they could get to me fairly easily right now and save themselves a load of trouble."

"David, there's no need to be like that. I said I was sorry."

"Be like what? I'm not being like anything. I'm just saying what you can't bring yourself to say."

"Okay, we need to both keep calm and maybe talk about this when we're less tired and emotional. We're both really worried about Candy so we're both on edge and—"

"You probably wouldn't care if she died, in fact, you'd probably be glad! You've never liked her much and you've never thought she was good enough for me, or Dad for that matter!"

"David!" Jill retorted. "How can you say that? Of course, I would care!"

"Tell me it's not true that you don't like her much and don't think she's good enough then."

"You know I can't. You know we both had similar opinions of her not that long ago. You used to think she was ditzy, clueless, shallow, and stupid, too, but you seem to have conveniently forgotten about that part. You might have had a major turnaround on your opinion, but I can't change mine quite so easily or quickly. She needs to prove to me that she can look after you in the most dangerous of situations and take care of you under circumstances where I can't. That's really difficult for me to deal with and for her to live up to, can't you see that?"

David folded his arms huffily, staring out of his window. They'd left the city behind and were driving through quiet, unlit back roads, woods either side of them. "I do see that, but I also see that she couldn't win no matter what she does. If she does a bad job she's not good enough, and if she's amazing and terrific you'll be jealous and want to get rid of her because I might like and admire her more than I do you."

Jill pursed her lips and bit her tongue. "I won't dignify that with a response, and I'm willing to overlook the fact that you're being a brat under the circumstances, but it's just you and me tonight and we really have to stick together and look out for one another. Let's not fall out before we even get home."

Something in her voice made David whip his head round and look at her with narrowed eyes. Whatever her words were saying, the tone revealed there was more behind them. Was it just because she was trying not to fight when it was all he wanted to do? He didn't know why he felt so angry but he wanted to explode, to stamp his feet and shake his fists, fling himself onto the ground in the type of temper tantrum that he didn't ever remember having as a young child, not even a toddler in the terrible twos, as adults always seemed to call it. For the first time, he *really* wanted to rage against this new life, to reject it, dismiss it, and deny its existence; to forget any of it had ever happened and have things back to normal as they'd been before. He knew he couldn't. He needed to address the issue at hand. "What's so specific about tonight? I get the feeling it's more than just Candy and Dad not being around."

Jill glanced at him from the corner of her eye, then looked quickly back to the road. "I wasn't going to tell you this, not tonight. I thought you'd had enough for one day and enough to cope with as it was."

"But?"

"I've had to change my mind. The mood you're in means I can't tell what you might do and I've got the feeling you don't have any trust or faith in me right now, so maybe you wouldn't do something I asked you to do. No matter if this is too much or not, you need to know right now. The reason I was so worried when I heard there was a disturbance at the shopping centre and the reason I called Candy to see if you were okay and nag you about getting home was because I'd just had a call from your granddad."

"There's nothing wrong is there? Is Grandma okay?"

"They're both fine, don't worry, but he did have some very bad news. He doesn't know how on earth it happened, but one of his old colleagues got in touch to advise him that Andrew has escaped from where he was being held by the Realm."

"Andrew! Do you think it could have been him that shot at us?"

"I don't know. I would imagine he'd be intent on revenge on us in addition to his original mission of eliminating a Gatekeeper, so it's more than likely he'd come back here, but I don't know how long ago he escaped so don't know if he'd be back here already or not. As I said, I wanted to put off telling you until morning but for your own safety, you've forced me into it. We have to stick together and be on our guard. I bet the Realm will probably have someone watching the house – especially now that word will have reached them about your Watcher being down and out – but just in case they don't, we have to be extra vigilant."

It was too much for the overwrought David, the final straw that pushed his emotions over the edge. Feeling a barrage of horrible words he knew he wouldn't mean pushing their way up into his throat and fighting their way to be released from his lips, he took advantage of the fact that Jill had pulled up at a give way sign and was waiting for a lone set of headlights to pass by before she pulled out and made her turn. He released his seatbelt, fumbled for the door handle, and flung himself out into the night. He stumbled but was on his feet and running, the tarmac giving way to a carpet of fallen leaves and twigs beneath his feet as he entered the woods.

"David! David! Come back!" Jill screamed.

He ignored his mother's call. He knew he was scared, confused, worried, upset, but all he could feel was furious with her. Furious for bringing Andrew into their lives and letting him get close to them. Furious that she might have been inadvertently and in a roundabout way responsible for Candy being shot and fighting for her life in intensive care. He knew his thoughts weren't fair, but he couldn't help but have them anyway. He would be better off alone, better away from her, somewhere he could think, somewhere he could calm down, somewhere he could regain some rationality and be a sensible human being again. For now, all he wanted to do was run.

He didn't really have any idea where he was going, only that he wanted out of sight and earshot of the car. He didn't know if his mum would start running through the woods after him but he suspected she won't. She would be more likely to go home, change, gather supplies such as ropes, first aid kits, and torches, and call together a search party to coordinate. Jill didn't go off half-cocked and was very good at looking at the bigger picture and playing the long game. He'd thought he was the same way. He hadn't considered himself a hothead, but now it looked as if it was something he was capable of being. The realisation surprised him.

His inner thoughts and the run slowly began to calm him and he reduced his pace to one where he was less likely to trip over a fallen branch and go flying, breaking his neck or ankle. Come time, his steady jog was further reduced to an easy lope until finally he came to a total halt, barely even winded thanks to Candy's meticulous training.

It was pitch in the woods. His eyes had adjusted to seeing only by the moonlight and stars, but he was frequently being plunged into darkness momentarily as thicker, darker clouds passed in front of the moon, blocking out her light. That was when he remembered he still had Candy's phone. He pulled it out of his pocket, thinking it was bound to have a torch app on it and even if it didn't, he could use the screen to light his way.

Unlocking it so that it came to life, he almost flung it away from him into the depth of the forest when he realised it was still covered in Candy's blood, both from her fingers and his own. He managed to overcome his initial reaction, holding on to the item that might end up being precious to him if something else bad happened. He wished he'd cleaned it off at the hospital after he'd used it to call his mum. He acknowledged that she'd been right later and that he'd been more or less in a daze at that point, numbed by the shock. His horror over Candy's dried blood meant that numbness and trance-like state was wearing off.

Everything came crashing in upon him then, how horrible he'd been to his mum, how selfish he was being running off when everyone had enough to deal with as it was, how scared he was that Candy wouldn't make it, how frightening it was thinking that the bullet might have been meant for him and he might be or should be the one lying in that hospital bed, and how hopelessly lost he'd gotten himself by charging off into the woods the way he had and running like a fool without paying the slightest bit of attention to which direction he was travelling in. He wanted to fall to his knees and sob, but he knew it wouldn't help anything and would only make him feel worse.

Instead, he sent a text to his mom, saying that he was sorry, that he was fine, that he just wanted some time alone to think and she shouldn't worry, definitely shouldn't bother Dad, and that he'd be home later. He knew it would hardly go any way at all to put her mind at rest but it was better than nothing. He could only hope that she would understand, forgive him, and not make herself ill with worry in the meantime. He should go back immediately but he didn't really want to. He actually did want that time alone to think.

Using the map app on the phone he pinpointed his location in the woods, glad that he had a fairly detailed knowledge of them through his hours upon hours spent here with Billie, and the times they'd spent drawing maps and plotting out routes. He could see that he wasn't far away from the part of the woods that he knew really well and knowing that made him feel much less vulnerable. Also, on seeing where he was, he knew exactly where he wanted to go.

Trying to ignore everything except putting one foot in front of the other, he used the compass he'd received as a gift from Billie to guide him to that special place where he wanted to be—standing in front of what he now thought of as the Hoogle tree. Reaching it, he couldn't actually see any in the darkness but he could sense their eyes watching him, could hear the odd whiffle and snuffle letting him know they were there. For reasons he didn't really understand and didn't care to think about at the moment, he found the sounds very comforting. He walked over, sat down at the base of the large tree, his back against the trunk, and closed his eyes. It wasn't long before there were too gentle thuds beside him and the weight of two small, scaly bodies pressed against him. He didn't need to open his eyes to know that it was two Hoogle that had come down to lay either side of him. He didn't know whether it was a security measure so they could keep an eye on him, if it were to share in his body heat, or even if it was to offer some sort of comfort to him. According to everyone else, the latter should be practically impossible, but after what he'd seen today, he was even surer that not only was it possible but it was very likely. He resisted the urge to reach out and lay his hands upon them or pull them closer to him. They weren't pets and he might just scare them away. Best to let whatever this was develop in its own time.

Feeling safer and more at ease than he'd done the entire day, David finally let his mind drift to the shocking news he'd been given just before he'd fled the car. How had it been possible for Andrew to escape? He'd never been to any of the Realm's facilities, had only met a handful of their operatives and then only briefly, but he'd seen and heard examples of how they handled everything and it always seemed so efficient, no room for error. He'd imaged that their version of a prison would be the highest tech, secure, impenetrable, and inescapable prison ever in existence. If he'd been wrong about that, then maybe he was wrong in everything he thought about the Realm itself. Perhaps it wasn't the almighty, all-powerful organisation that he'd thought it was. Still, that was a consideration for another day, another time. Right now, he needed to worry about what Andrew's escape meant for them all in the immediate future. Could it really be possible that it was Andrew that had shot at him and Candy today? Could he be here already? That thought would actually be a comfort. Candy had warned him there would be more Seekers after him than other Gatekeepers, but she'd spoken about it as a possibility for the future, something that shouldn't be snowballing as word spread quite so soon. Whoever had fired that gun must have known the odds of getting caught were high and risked spending a lifetime in jail to take that shot regardless. If they'd managed to evade capture, there was still ballistics, gun registrations, and all sorts of other clever methods to track down the weapon and hopefully the shooter. David maybe couldn't trust the Realm as much as he'd believed, but he could certainly trust police procedures. Having several Seekers that were that desperate to take him out would be more worrying than believing it was Andrew. He almost laughed aloud at the idea of having Andrew after him again being the best of his options.

He didn't think he was in any immediate danger tonight. Either Andrew wasn't there yet or he'd be in hiding after firing that gun, knowing the hunt would be in full swing. Even if Andrew was crazy enough to keep on going, he would likely be hanging around the hospital, thinking that they'd all still be there. The worst case would be that he would be at the house, but Mum knew to be on her guard and she'd already said the Realm would likely be watching and ready to recapture him if he showed up there. Everyone was safe for now, everyone was being looked after, he could just keep his eyes closed and relax for a few minutes, the Hoogle would look out for him…

CHAPTER TWENTY

"Well, isn't this a turn up for the books."

David's eyes shot open, instantly awake from the deep sleep he'd fallen into, the two Hoogle at his sides also leaping to their feet, one of them hissing. David would recognise that voice anywhere. After all, he'd spent an awfully long time hearing it and believing it came from a father figure and a good friend. He hadn't expected to hear it here tonight. His surprise must have shown on his face.

Andrew laughed. "Shocked to see me? I can't really blame you. I'm still surprised at how it all came about too, can't quite believe my luck if I'm honest. Finding you out here isn't just dumb luck, though, I'd have staked money on that at some point even if I hadn't been following you and Jill home from the hospital. Still busy mooning over that friend of yours and now all upset about that silly bimbo, Candy. Stands to reason you would run for the place that reminds you of Billie the most, the place where you feel safest.

Well, guess what? Your sanctuary isn't going to be your sanctuary tonight, never again actually."

In the light of the moon, David saw a glint of steel flash in the hand that Andrew was waving around as he spoke. Although his speech was cheerful, gleeful even, Andrew's grin was macabre, and combined with the hard, cold look in his eyes, made him appear completely unhinged. David knew he was in massive trouble, especially when Andrew's hand went still and he saw the gun nestled comfortably there.

From previous experience, there was no point in trying to talk Andrew down or reason with him. He had his own agenda and wouldn't be swayed from it for any reason; David understood that this time at least, not that it helped him in any way. With Candy out of action, he was a bit of a sitting duck. Knowing that he didn't have his Watcher to protect him, the Realm may have supplied temporary protectors but he'd blown that for himself when he'd had his little temper tantrum and ran off on his own. Whatever was about to happen would entirely be his own fault. Somehow, accepting that made it easier to face.

He could feel the Hoogle dropping down from the tree all around him. He had the feeling that they wanted to help but he didn't have a clue if they knew what they'd be facing. No doubt, the gun was fully loaded and Andrew would have more bullets with him to reload as often as he needed. Anyone who'd escaped from the Realm's prison would know how to prepare for a mission like this. The Hoogle didn't seem to be a violent species, seemed reluctant to hurt anything, and they might never have seen a gun before. It was more than likely that the moment it went off they would scatter and scarper. David hoped they would. In fact, he wished they would do it now.

"Stop it," he told the Hoogle firmly. "Go on back up to your tree. Get out of here."

"Who are you talking to?" Andrew asked, his curiosity evident as he took a few steps forward until he was only a few feet in front of David. "Had to make up some imaginary friends since you lost the only one you had?"

David rose to his feet slowly, not wanting to startle Andrew into anything but hoping that he was distracted enough not to care too much. "I said get out of here. You can't help and I don't want any of you getting hurt. Shoo. All of you."

Andrew laughed. "Ah, I get it. It's a bluff! You want me to think you've got some help; that you've got something here that I can't see. Well, I'm not falling for it. The only way there could be anything here is if there was an open gate, and I'm not stupid enough to believe that a Gatekeeper would be lying sleeping if there were an open gate nearby. Nice try, though. Makes sense that you would try to use your brains to find a way out of this since you're such a wimpy little nerd. They're not going to be much good to you now, though. Brains aren't much of a match for a gun, especially when it blows them out."

"I don't suppose *anything* would be a match against a gun," David said pointedly, trying to alert the Hoogle to the level of danger they were facing, not even considering the fact that they probably didn't understand him or have a clue what was going on. "It's a very precise and deadly weapon."

"Very true, and you're about to learn all about that first hand."

David had felt the shift in the mood of the Hoogle while the exchange had been taking place, felt their intensity build, felt the gathering excitement in the air.

Andrew raised the gun and pointed it at David's head.

Looking down, the barrel of a gun was something David had read about in books but never thought he'd have to experience. It was far more terrifying than he could have ever believed. It was tiny but looked massive, that dark centre cavernous and the length never ending. It chilled him to the bone. The outcome of this night seemed inevitable. He was filled with regrets for those that he'd leave behind and the job he'd be leaving undone, knowing that this was mostly his own fault. He wanted to hang his head, he wanted to shiver in fear, he wanted to drop to his knees and beg for his life. He was determined that he wasn't going to do any of those things. He might be about to die but he was going to die as a Gatekeeper—proud, and in the line of duty, a soldier of sorts, charged with protecting his world a gate at a time, rather than his country, battle by battle. He squared his shoulders, raised his head, and stared Andrew straight in the eye.

The creep of a man laughed again, as if delighted by the futile defiance, as if pleased that the shy, quiet, frightened little boy had finally found some courage in the last few moments of his life. David let him have his fun. What difference did it make?

The Hoogle swarmed around his feet, one of them reaching out to touch his hand. He reached for those long bony talons in return, took it, and squeezed, thanking it for the moral support and the caring. Not having the time to learn more about these strange, fascinating little creatures was only one of his many regrets. The hand tugged. David ignored it, wanting to make sure he held Andrew's gaze right up until the very last moment, hoping that the look in his eye as he pulled the trigger would haunt the slime bag forever. Andrew probably wasn't capable of remorse but if there was as much as the slimmest possibility, then David wanted to give it every chance. The claw-like hand tugged again. He heard a clicking sound from the gun that echoed throughout the wood as Andrew cocked the weapon. Finally, David realised what it was that the Hoogle was trying to draw his attention to with the tugs.

Out of the corner of his eye, he saw that the visual disturbances typical of an oncoming migraine had begun to build. Both hope and fear flared within him, his mind racing with a tumult of thoughts. The gate was in the process of opening. Would it happen before Andrew pulled the trigger? If it did, would it help him any anyway? In that split second, everything had changed. No longer was there just one outcome, although there simply wasn't the time to rationalise what the others could possibly be. He only needed to stall Andrew for a few more brief seconds. From then on in, it was all an unknown, but an unknown was better than certain death.

"Killing me tonight is all well and good. I'm sure you'll be heralded as a hero for it, but it won't do your cause much good in the long run, will it? There are still thousands, maybe millions of others just like me doing the same job, and new generations waiting to take our place when the Seekers fail to eradicate every one of us and our bloodlines. You'll never do it."

Antagonising him was risky but he thought Andrew would see through playing to his ego in a more direct manner such as flattering questions. Perhaps a heated discussion would distract him if he could enrage him just enough. Unfortunately, Andrew refused to bite.

"Oh, we'll do it all right," he said, his tone and manner nonchalant. "And it all starts right here with you tonight. You're no ordinary Gatekeeper, David, just too good for your own good. Taking you out will further our cause no end, not least by the boost of confidence it will give us all; Just knowing you can be eradicated easily will have every Seeker buoyed and fired up, doubling their efforts. Word will spread in no time; trust me. I might even take a little trophy to show off when I become the stuff of legend for being the one to take you down. Not sure what yet. Maybe that silly little compass that you like so much, but I'll have plenty of time to decide afterwards."

David had been trying not to be a total amateur and keep on looking at the gate to see how its formation was coming along. He didn't want to alert Andrew to the fact that anything unusual was happening, even though both he and the Hoogle were highly aware of it. He didn't need to look in its direction to know the moment it actually came into full existence. He heard and felt the crackle and fizzle in the air, heard the whoosh and pop, and saw the flash of bright light that illuminated several feet of the forest all around him. The disturbance hummed quietly for a moment before it settled. David knew there was a route to a different world less than a handful of feet away to his left. The question was, how best to make use of that in this situation?

Andrew wasn't going to give him time to think about it. "Anyway, enough chat. You did that last time, didn't you, outfoxed me by keeping me talking too long? Well, I'm not making that mistake again, and my arm's getting tired of holding this gun at your head. Wish I could say it was nice knowing you, David, but it really wasn't, and you should think yourself lucky that I'm making it quick and final with a headshot and not making you suffer like that blonde idiot of a Watcher. Getting rid of the pair of you will be the greatest moment of my life."

The gunshot exploded through the quiet of the forest, the sound alien and deafening. Birds screeched and took to the wing in fright, their flapping and squawking filling the air as much as their bodies blocking out the light of the moon. Smaller animals went tearing off through the thicket, while deer crashed through it, snorting in terror. All of this happened as David turned and ran a few steps before flinging his small body with all the energy he could muster.

He hadn't needed to be careful not to give Andrew any subconscious clues regarding his intention as he hadn't planned it, might even have dismissed the idea if he'd had a second to think it through. As it was, the bullet missed, hurtling through the air, whizzing through the place where David's head had been only a fraction of a second before, and embedded itself into the thick trunk of the Hoogle tree.

Furious but undeterred, Andrew whirled to the side, the gun still raised, expecting to see David running for his life, more than prepared to pull the trigger again. What he saw made his mouth fall open in surprise. He caught a quick glimpse of David leaping through the air then completely disappearing from sight as if he'd just puffed out of existence. Frantically looking in all directions, Andrew couldn't see him anywhere. David had vanished. His arm fell to his side. For now, he was defeated. There was only one explanation—David had done what was forbidden to all Gatekeepers, he jumped through a gate.

Chapter Twenty-One

"What do you mean disappeared?" William hissed, his eyes flicking in the direction of the sleeping Candy.

"Exactly that," Jill said, defensive and haughty, already blaming herself with no need for anyone else to do it for her. She was too tried to keep her voice low, considerate of her location. "He leapt out of the car, ran off into the woods, and we can't find him anywhere. There was nothing I could do; I was at a junction at the time."

"Why didn't I hear about this sooner?"

"Because the woman you love is seriously injured. She needed you and you needed to be by her side. I was doing everything that could be done anyway. I thought I had everything under control."

"Well, obviously you didn't."

"No, obviously not." Jill tried to be annoyed but her voice broke and she burst into tears, sitting down heavily on the chair in Candy's room and covering her face with her hands. "I'm sorry. It seems I did everything wrong."

William instantly felt guilty for giving her a hard time. He rushed to her, hunkering down in front of her and placing his hands on her shoulders. "Jill, look at me. You didn't do anything wrong. You made every decision based on what you thought was the best thing to do at the time and that's all anyone can ever do. No one's blaming you. Here, blow your nose and tell me everything from start to finish."

Jill blew with the tissue he offered her, sniffed, and wiped at her eyes with her fingertips. "Maybe we should go somewhere else. I don't want to disturb Candy. She needs her rest to recover."

"She's still heavily sedated. I don't think she'll wake up. They only finally let me in here because they felt sorry for me and were fed up of me looking like a lost sheep in the waiting room."

"If you're sure…"

"I am."

She told him everything that had happened from the night before; every detail of the conversation that had taken place in the car before David had run away. William listened intently and when she came to a halt, he reached out and stroked one of the deep scratches on her cheek with his thumb. "How did you get this?"

"I tried to chase after him. It didn't do me any good. He's smaller, faster, and has spent hours in those woods. I just kept on running into branches in the dark and falling over roots buried in the ground. I tried my best but had to give up. Without a light of some kind, I knew I was going to end up breaking something and being stuck out there, and then I wouldn't have been any use to anyone. That's when I went home, got changed, gathered supplies, and called every single person we know. I was out there all night and most of this morning. There was no way he could have got further than the ground we covered. I just don't understand why we didn't find him. That's when I knew I had to come and tell you what was going on."

William rose, beginning to pace in the confines of the private room in intensive care, tapping his lip with his index finger. "I take it you did check that he hadn't come home and gone to bed in the meantime?"

"Yes. I'd left several notes all over the house telling him to call me if he got in when I wasn't there, and I went back to check before I came here, just in case he still wasn't talking to me."

"I don't think that'll be the case. You know that wouldn't be like him, none of this really is. Sounds to me like he was just a bit overwhelmed and didn't know how to feel or react. I'm sure he'll be fine. You know what he and Billie were like, always exploring those woods. He's probably in a cave, a hollowed out trunk, or up in some treehouse or something that you've missed. I'm sure he'll come home when he's ready."

Jill chewed on her nail. She could taste the polish in her mouth, felt it chip, felt the nail split and break. She glanced guiltily at Candy, knowing she would be horrified at the damage she'd done to her always-perfect work. She wondered why on earth she was focusing on something so stupid at a time like this. There was one vital piece of information she was withholding from William, and it was time to come clean. Hesitantly, falteringly, she told him about Andrew.

William's face first went red with fury at the mention of the man's name, then it turned a chalky shade of white. He clutched at the nearest piece of furniture, using it to steady his balance. "Why didn't you tell me that before? That changes everything."

"Does it, though," Jill said, her tone desperate. "Does it really? I've been trying to think it through. If we assume that Andrew was the one that shot Candy, then we know where he was and at what time. He would know that the police would be searching the vicinity, so he would have fled or gone into hiding. We coming to the hospital was obvious, but why would *he* come here? We'd all be together, police would be guarding Candy, and it's a busy, crowded place with people around all the time. He couldn't get to us here. I decided that he most likely would have gone straight to our house. That really was his only sensible option, wasn't it?"

Hope had crept into William's eyes and now shone there. "I think you might be right! It would've been stupid of him to follow us to where he couldn't get to us. He's bound to have gone to the house and David never made it that far. No one could have anticipated him running off into the woods like that. He's probably safer there than anywhere."

"Yes, exactly! And the Realm will be watching our house and will recapture Andrew soon. They're bound to have people on it, and on trying to watch out for David since Candy's down. I'm surprised they haven't sent a replacement yet."

"Maybe they tried but no one's been home. Doesn't matter; what's important is that there doesn't seem to be any way Andrew could have got to David. That's a relief."

"It is. He's likely safe in the woods just like you said and will make his way home as soon as he's hungry, cold, or just had enough and wants his nice warm bed."

"Billie wasn't safe in the woods."

The slurred, groggy voice startled them, causing them both to jump. They'd almost forgotten she was even in the room with them.

"Candy, you're awake!" William cried.

"Almost," she said, grimacing as she tried to sit up.

"Whoa, careful there, take it easy." William rushed over, steadying her and helping her sit up the rest of the way, propping the pillows behind her. "How do you feel?"

"Sore, dizzy, fuzzy, thirsty, but most of all, worried."

"How long were you awake?"

"The sound of Jill crying more or less woke me up, although I couldn't move or speak at first."

"The sedative," William explained. "They wanted to keep you out for the count so your body had nothing to do but heal."

"Whatever, doesn't matter. What matters is that David's missing. I need to get out of here."

"Oh no, no way, you can't. Won't hear of it. You're staying put until the doctors release you. David will be fine. We'll find him or he'll come home on his own soon."

"That's what everyone thought about Billie."

Jill had come to the edge of the bed. "That's what you said a moment ago. You don't really think this could be like Billie, do you?" The question was barely more than a frightened whisper.

"Nobody actually knows what happened to her so we can't say, can we?"

Candy examined everything she was hooked up, her frustration evident. "William, can you buzz for the nurse, please. I need to get all this stuff off of me."

"Of course…wait, no! Why would I do that?"

"I told you. So I can get out of here."

"And I've already told you that you're not going anywhere. In case you've forgotten, you were shot recently."

"That was yesterday, almost twenty-one hours ago," Candy said with a glance at the wall clock. "Long enough. Besides, you said I've done nothing but sleep since then so my body's had plenty of time to start healing."

"Rubbish! You haven't even spoken to a doctor yet, whereas we have."

"So tell me then," Candy said, folding her arms and glowering at him. "What did they say about my condition?"

William could be equally as stubborn when he wanted to be. "I'm saying nothing. You'll take the doctors more seriously. You can wait until they examine you and talk to them yourself."

Candy turned to Jill. "Jill, you'll tell me, won't you?"

Jill looked at William and shrugged apologetically. "I'm sorry, but David has to come first. Candy, you were shot in the stomach, the bullet hitting your liver. They've sewn you up inside and out, but there's a risk of further internal bleeding and infection setting in. They had to give you a massive blood transfusion, so you're very weak and they want to keep on fluids, sedatives, pain relief, and probably antibiotics for a while."

"That's it?"

"Yes, at least it was when the nurse first spoke to us immediately after your surgery."

"Then what are we waiting for! If the infection hasn't set in by now it's not going to, and the liver is a rejuvenating organ anyway. I learned that at the academy. It'll replace any damaged bits by itself, mine quicker than most; I'm a Watcher remember? Now, if you don't call a nurse to come and take all these tubes and wires out of me, so help me I'll yank them all out myself!"

CHAPTER TWENTY-TWO

'David! David, help me, I'm lost! David!'

The voice was faint, distant, yet the desperation and loneliness within it was clear.

'David, please help me. Please find me.'

"I'm coming!"

David jerked awake, surprised to find himself outdoors in a dawn that was just turning into morning. He listened carefully, trying to hear the voice again. All he could hear was the chirping of birds, the rustling of leaves, and the occasional lazy buzz of an insect. It had been so real. He could have sworn that he'd heard Billie calling for him. With a disappointed sigh, he decided it must have been only in his dreams. He rubbed at his eyes and took in his surroundings. As he discovered that he'd been sleeping on a bed of leaves at the base of a tree, the events of the night before began to come back to him. He sat there for a moment, letting it all sink in and become clear in his memories. He allowed the range of emotions to flood him as he recalled each event, figuring it would be best to let himself experience it and get it out of the way. Once it was over, he could focus on the here and now. The reality of his current situation was that he'd now done both things he'd been told he must never ever do. The first, to tell anyone not involved about this secret world, and the second, to go through a gate. He was two for two on breaking the rules and it didn't feel good at all. *I'll just have to deal with the fact that I'm a bad Gatekeeper when I get back,* he decided, rising to his feet. *That's if I ever do get back.*

Everywhere he looked, he saw exactly what he expected to see; a forest like any other, one almost exactly the same as the one he'd spent his childhood playing in and exploring. He had to remember that this wasn't those woods. It might be made up of a fragment of his own planet that had gone hurtling off into space, but just as the earth had developed in its own way, each of those fragments had also developed very differently. Each and every one was unique, and what was there depended on what life had been upon it, what had survived and what had died during both the blast and the time as a solitary rock, and what other elements were drawn to it and joined it as it floated around in space. It was what had been happening during, and what had happened after, that made it a world in its own right. Every single one was like a twin of the earth, torn from it in infancy, raised by different people in a completely different environment, a different culture, a different time, sharing the same DNA, but having it altered beyond recognition. Nurture, not nature. That was the logical part, the sensible part that David's brain could follow and work out. If he'd been born in a different time and place, he'd be a different person too, let alone if he'd been raised by different parents. It made sense. It was how they'd all kept that connection to the earth that puzzled him, how they'd all stuck close or maybe even made their way back here, and how the gates had formed and what they really were. Those were the massive questions that seemed to have no answer. He wasn't sure if the human race as it existed right now even had the capability of figuring that out. It was too big for our brains, too much to comprehend. Besides, he supposed it didn't really matter right now. The part he needed to focus on was the first. He needed to remember that things might feel familiar but they very definitely were not. That knowledge might help keep him alive, provided he found his way back through the gate in a hurry.

He pulled out his compass, hoping for a different result than the one he'd had last night. Nothing had changed. The needle was still spinning and jumping wildly, unable to settle on a direction, unable to tell him where he needed to go. Candy's smartphone app had proven to be useless too. In fact, the entire phone was useless. It would turn on, it still had battery power, but that was it. The words 'No Service' would pop up on the screen and the phone wouldn't do anything else, not even run the applications that should have been available without a service provider. It was just another mystery of the gates and worlds. He didn't even bother trying it today. He needed to save the battery in case he needed it when he got back through the gate.

He tried again to recall his exact movements of the night before. He remembered that he'd taken a flying leap through, landing heavily on his shoulder, jarring it badly. He'd scrabbled to his feet and ran, afraid that Andrew would be furious enough or crazy enough to follow him through, or that he could simply shoot him through the open gate. Using something he'd seen in a film once, he'd zigged and zagged, dodged and wove as he went, making it hard for the bullet to hit him. He'd thought he was being clever, and maybe in a way, he was. He hadn't been shot anyway. However, by the time he was sure Andrew wasn't following and that he was out of range of the gun and stopped, he'd completely lost his bearings. He'd immediately checked the compass to see if he could determine in which direction he'd ran but found it misbehaving again, no help at all. He'd carefully turned, and keeping to the shadow of trees, he had crept along in what he thought was back in the direction he'd come, hoping to see the shimmering and flashing circle of light around the gate. He'd seen nothing, heard nothing, and felt nothing. The obvious explanation was that the gate had closed. If that was the case, then all he had to do was survive until it opened again so he could go home. That might not be too difficult if he kept his head down and stayed quiet. The only thing that had come through this gate last time was a few large insects that had given Candy a nasty reaction, nothing more serious than that. Maybe there wasn't anything else. Maybe there was, but maybe it lived far away from the gate. He could only hope.

Feeling as if there was nothing much else he could do that night, he'd laid down beneath a large tree on a thick, soft bed of fallen leaves and allowed the whispers of the wind through the leaves to lull him to sleep.

The next thing he remembered was hearing Billie call to him but that hadn't been real, only a figment of hope and wishful thinking created by his subconscious in his dreams. Now it was full daylight. He felt less exhausted and a little rested, but still had absolutely no clue what to do next. He decided he might as well sit back down and think things over again.

Giving a few seconds consideration to all his body's functions, he decided he didn't feel any different from usual and everything seemed to be working normally. That was good, as was the amount of time he'd survived here already. It meant things like air quality and composition, gravity, temperature, and lots of other things essential for human survival that he always took for granted, were similar to earth. Taking monsters that might want to kill him or eat him out of the equation gave him three days without water before dehydration got him. He wasn't sure if he could risk drinking the water even if he could find any, nor did he know if the gate would open again within three days. Then, an even more terrible, awful thought struck him.

What if he couldn't see the gate?

He tried not to hyperventilate as he admitted the truth of it to himself. In his own world, he was a Gatekeeper; one of a special few that could perceive what went on beyond the normal spectrum of human senses. What if here, he wasn't? What if he was just one of those ordinary people who could walk past a gate or the monsters and see nothing? The gate could be open right now, only a foot or so away, and he would never know. In a wood that looked the same but wasn't, he could spend a lifetime trying to hit upon an invisible gate. That would mean he would never get home. That would mean he would be stuck here forever, or for the rest of life, which, all things considered, might not be very long.

***

On the other side of the gate, Andrew sat on the forest floor, staring at what he believed was the very last spot he'd seen David. He'd grown a little disorientated when he'd turned in all directions looking for him, but he was sure he had it now. The little wimp had to have gone through a gate, and that meant he had to come back through it, too. Of course, Andrew was no fool. He might not be able to see anything, but Seekers had heard plenty of stories about the types of things that lived beyond the gates. There was every possibility that David wouldn't come back at all. That was even better; he wouldn't have a body to worry about hiding or burying. He would wait for two or three days and if David hadn't reappeared by then, he would assume he was a goner. Then he would just have that Watcher to deal with, just because she irritated him and had thwarted him once before. That was still irking him. She was so dumb that she never should have been able to get the better of him or figure out what he was. No point in worrying about it now, though, things were back on track and were going even better than he could have imagined.

CHAPTER TWENTY-THREE

"What a palaver," Candy grumbled. "You'd think no one had ever signed themselves out of the hospital before. If I had to sign one more form, I was going to scream. What was with all that?"

"It's because it's against everyone's advice and our better judgement," William replied, equally as irritated but with Candy rather than the hospital. "This is ridiculous. I know you're worried about David, but why does it have to be you? We could have asked Geoff to appeal directly to the Realm or something."

"The Realm should have been contacted ages ago," Candy said. "I have like a million things to say to them, would've said most of it already if I had my phone and the numbers I need."

"You don't have them memorised?"

"Who the heck memorises numbers these days? No one has to, that's what smartphones are for. Can I get out of this stupid chair yet?"

"A few more minutes and we'll be outside."

"This is so dumb. Didn't one of those fifty billion forms I signed clear them of any liability?"

"Quite a few of them, I would imagine."

"So they can't force me to use this thing then. Stop and let me get out."

"Oh, for heaven's sake, no I will not," William retorted. You'll sit there until we get to the car."

"Well, hurry it up a bit at least."

William didn't really mind Candy being snappy with him, or the bickering that was happening between them. They weren't really annoyed at one another, and they were both using it as a temporary distraction from the bigger issue—David's welfare. They both knew that with every passing moment, the odds of something bad happening to him increased.

Finally, the automatic glass doors were in sight. They both took a deep breath of air as they slid open and William pushed the chair outside.

"I don't know why they always have hospitals so hot and stuffy," he said. "I know people are ill and they don't want them getting cold, but surely the place being that stifling only breeds germs."

"Never mind that, we're outside so we can use the mobile. Call Jill and ask if he's turned up yet."

William wheeled the chair to an out of the way spot and fumbled around in his pockets for his phone. After turning it on and impatiently willing it to hurry up and go through its boot system, he dialled Jill's number. She'd gone ahead earlier, leaving him to stay with Candy, who was too anxious to find out what was happening with the search to stick around through the arguments with the doctors and nurses over her discharge. He leapt straight in when he heard her answer. "Hi, any news?"

"Nothing. He's not at home and the search parties have still come up empty handed. Dad hasn't heard anything about Andrew being apprehended either so we can only assume that he's still on the loose."

"Well?"

Candy was standing beside William, trying to get her ear close enough to the phone to hear what was being said, having taken advantage of stopping to abandon the chair. William shook his head, letting her know there was no news.

"Tell Jill to meet us at Sycamore Crescent, down at the wooden gate that leads into the woods. Does she know where I mean?" Candy said.

William relayed the message and nodded. "Okay, soon as we can." He hung up. "I suppose I know where I'm going, I just don't know why."

"I'll tell you both at once when we get there," Candy replied.

It had to be good enough for William. He didn't want to press Candy too much. She insisted on walking across the car park and by the time she reached the car, she was looking pale and pinched again. He resisted nagging and tried to remember that she was putting herself at risk for his son. He was thankful, but she would understand that without him saying a word. He let her rest in silence as he drove. She had a touch more colour in her cheeks again by the time they'd reached their destination.

Sycamore Crescent was a quiet cul-de-sac in suburbia not far from where they lived. William drove to where there was a small parking area that could accommodate five or six cars if they were parked carefully enough. Off the parking area was a wooden gate that gave way to a path into the woods, nothing but dense forest for miles after that. It was the nearest entrance into the woodland from their house, the one that Billie and David most often used. William saw Jill's car already parked there. He pulled in alongside as she got out, pulling a large and heavy looking backpack onto her shoulders while she waited for them to exit their car.

"What's our plan?" Jill asked.

"Best ask Candy, I haven't a clue," William said.

Both turned to look at Candy, questioning.

"I don't think David's changed that much as a person since this whole thing began," Candy began. "But there are things about him that are different, or maybe what I mean is that there's more to him than there used to be. Anyway, I'm probably the one that knows those new things the best and I've got a feeling I know where he might have headed when he ran away. Whether he's still there is anyone's guess but it's worth a shot. I just don't think I can make it there alone, or that trying would be smart. Will you trust my judgement and come with me?"

"You don't even need to ask me that," William said.

"Me neither," Jill added. "When it comes to David, I trust you'll do whatever you think is best for him, and if you think you know where he might have gone, then what are we waiting for."

"Thanks, guys. It's this way."

They made their way single file through the kissing gate and into the woods.

William wrapped his arm around Candy's waist, supporting her to conserve her energy. "So where are we going?" he asked her.

"I can't really explain, and there won't be anything for us to see when we get there either, except, hopefully, David. That's why I needed you to trust me. If he's not there, then it's not going to look like anything except another tree among hundreds."

"Fair enough, but if there's nothing to see, how will you know it's the right tree?"

"From the amount of times I've been there…"

William and Jill sensed she was reluctant to say much more and that talking was using up energy she didn't have to spare. They fell silent, simply following when she veered off the path and led them through the trees. Her movements were slowing down and her breathing growing more laboured by the time she halted. She took a moment to catch her breath before speaking, her voice low. "It's not far ahead, but I want us to go very quietly, just in case."

"In case what?" Jill murmured back.

"Dunno really, just trusting my gut. Stay behind me, but please stay close. I know I'm not up to much right now."

Candy crept forward, heading for the tree where the Hoogle lived. She couldn't see or hear them, but coming here nearly every day to check on the gate, she not only knew the route but recognised the tree too. She stopped dead in her tracks and waved her hand at Jill and William to halt them too when she saw the cross-legged figure sitting staring intently at the tree. It wasn't whom she'd been expecting to see. She turned around. 'Andrew,' she silently mouthed to them.

They backed away slowly and carefully, keeping to the wettest fallen leaves so their footsteps didn't crunch, and trying to avoid any twigs or branches that might snap beneath their weight. Andrew seemed oblivious to anything and everything, solely focused on the spot in front of him. Candy hadn't missed the gun he held in the hand that was resting on one of his knees. It filled her with a sense of dread, her wounds aching at the very sight of it. She didn't stop until she felt they were far enough away to talk in whispers without being heard.

"What do we do, Candy?" Jill whispered.

"I don't know. Give me a minute, Jill; I need to think this through. There's something in my head, something that's trying to come to me. I've got a feeling it should be obvious but I'm missing it."

"Maybe if we knew more we could help." William's tone was gentle and encouraging. "What made you think David might be here?"

Candy hesitated only a moment, weighing up her options before deciding that talking was best. "A tree where lots of Hoogle live."

"Hoogle? Those horrible, drooling creatures with the teeth, claws, and bright green snot? I've heard all about them," Jill said with a shudder. "Why on earth would he want to go where they live?"

"Way too much to explain, you'll just have to trust me again. The other thing that's here is—oh!"

"Candy, what is it?"

What popped into Candy's head chilled her to the bone and filled her with a fear far greater than the one seeing the gun had induced. She looked at William and Jill's worried faces and wondered if she should even tell them. She had to. She needed them, and she needed them to know what they might be dealing with. "The way Andrew was so focused on the empty space was weird. I got the feeling he was watching and waiting for something, and I think I just figured what it is out. He's not looking in quite the right place but almost. The other thing that's here is a gate. Don't panic and don't make a sound, but I think he might have seen David go through it."

Jill clamped her hand over her own mouth to stifle the squeal that threatened to burst forth. If there was one lesson that every parent of a Gatekeeper knew to teach them it was never to go through a gate. David knew that. He must have been desperate. Had he already been hurt? What would have been waiting for him on the other side? Was he even alive?

"Jill, I can read everything that's running across your mind in your face. Stop it. We need to stay calm and think the best, not the worst. We need to neutralise Andrew before that gate opens. We have to assume that it isn't going to open right now, but it will at some point, and that David will walk through it completely unharmed when it does, do you hear me?

It needs to be us waiting for him when he does, not Andrew, so pull yourself together! I can't do this alone."

She glowered at Jill, her heart aching for her but knowing she needed to be stern. Eventually, Jill nodded and Candy released her from her glare, trusting that whatever happened from now on she would rise to it and stay focused. The only thing left to do was figure out a plan she could work with in her current physical condition. The odds weren't in her favour and nothing was ideal, but she would have to do whatever she could. "What's in that backpack, anything useful? Hand it over."

Jill shrugged it off her shoulders and held it out to Candy.

William was there in a flash, taking it and laying it on the ground. "It's heavy. I'll look through it for you. Coil of rope, water, cereal bars, energy drinks, a map, first aid kit, blanket, blow up pillow, insect spray, antihistamine, duct tape… duct tape?" William looked at Jill curiously.

Jill blushed. "Yes. Everyone always says it has a thousand and one uses so when I saw the roll, I thought it couldn't hurt to bring it along. Maybe one of those thousand uses would be the one that saved David's life or helped me not get lost in the woods."

William shrugged to concede the point. It was incredibly useful stuff. "Fair enough. That's about it, apart from some glucose tablets, hand sanitizer, and a toilet roll. Only you would bring that on a hike, Jill."

"Leave her alone, it's a pretty good woods survival kit," Candy said, about to raise her hand to offer Jill a high five but thinking better of it when she felt her stitches and dressings pull. "If I wasn't hurt, I'd say I'd take the rope, climb that tree closest to him, crawl along a branch until I was directly overhead, then drop down and get the rope around him. As it is, even I could get up there, I'd never be quiet enough, and dropping down would hurt so much I wouldn't be able to finish the job."

"I could do it," William offered.

"No. He has a gun, remember. If you miss or mistime, you give him the chance to use that on you and it would be point blank range. No chance of survival that close."

"Then none of us are doing it. We'll just have come up with something else. Why don't we just call the Realm?"

"I thought about that too," Jill jumped in.

"So did I, guys, but I don't have the number as I don't have my phone, and I'm not sure if they could find us and get here in time anyway. The gate could already be open and David might appear back here any second, thinking he'd be safe now. Jill, you could call your father and ask him to make the necessary calls so we know they're coming eventually, but we don't really know what happens on the other side of these gates. Maybe David will think weeks have passed and there would be no way Andrew would still be here. Maybe it'll open and we won't see the gate but we might see David through it, and so would Andrew. There are too many unknowns to waste time waiting for reinforcements. We need to do something now."

Candy chewed on her bottom lip, thinking hard, the noises of the woods providing a soundtrack to her thoughts. Hearing a buzzing nearby, Candy subconsciously rubbed at the spot on her neck where she'd been stung by the insect that had come through the gate. Her reaction brought the incident to mind. Those insects hadn't bothered David, yet one had determinedly chased her. The spot was directly down from behind her ear, where she sprayed her perfume. Could that have been it? She always wore fruity or sweet scents. She grinned as an idea began to form. "Guys, insects like sweet things, don't they?"

"Yes, they do."

"So they'd be attracted to them and if there's one place you'd find lots of insects it would be in the woods, right?" She might not have the creatures David had described to her to work with but normal ones were bad enough, especially in large numbers.

Jill's grin was starting to form, seeing where Candy was going with this. "Okay, I think I get it. We have the energy drinks, which are really sweet and sticky. He'd be inundated with ants, flies, bees, wasps, gnats, and every other species that lives here. That would provide the perfect distraction for us to disarm him and tie him up. The only question is how to cover him in the stuff without him seeing us and shooting us. Even if we poured it down on top of him from the tree, he's going to feel it."

"Covering him in it would be ideal but maybe we don't have to. Close might be enough, like when you have a picnic and the food is on the table or rug, but the wasps are hovering around you trying to locate the source of the nice scents. All we need is him distracted *enough*."

They settled down to discuss the plan. The urge to act quickly at odds with Candy's determination to ensure that they'd thought it all through properly and that nothing would go wrong.

CHAPTER TWENTY-FOUR

David hugged his knees to his chest and rested his chin on them. He wasn't sure what to do. He was hungry but that wasn't a problem, not yet. What was more worrying was how thirsty he was. The body could go without food for quite a while, but the average for survival without water was three days. He was torn. Should he stay where he thought the gate was, hope that it opened in time, and that he would actually see it when it did, or should he go in search of something to drink, even if it meant getting lost? If he did find a stream or something, could he risk drinking, *would* he risk it? Would a fast death from water poisonous to him be preferable to the slower dehydration? It wasn't a question he'd ever thought he would have to ask himself. He wished he had someone to talk it over with and hear their opinion.

"Well, there isn't anybody, so tough luck, David. You're on your own this time." He felt a bit silly talking aloud to himself but at the same time, he couldn't quite shake the feeling that he wasn't. It was crazy but he felt as if he had a companion; that nearby, there was a friend and not an enemy. He tried not to pay much heed, knowing it was probably wishful thinking. Besides, his own voice had been comforting. What did it matter if he felt silly anyway? He might be in a place where not another living soul spoke English, or even human, and he wouldn't find any answers sitting here.

Asking himself what Candy would do, he knew she would be proactive. If she were a Gatekeeper in his situation, she would already have searched for monsters to find out if she could see them, thus answering the question of whether she would be able to see the gate or not. She might have left a trail Hansel and Gretel style to find her way back to this area, or maybe tried to memorise the route. As for the water, she'd want to know one way or another as soon as possible. Why prolong uncertainty and suffer unnecessarily? Of course, he couldn't be certain Candy would come to those conclusions. Maybe they were his own decisions but he needed to put her name to them, lacking the courage of his own convictions. Either way, it helped.

He leapt to his feet and began to gather twigs and stones that he felt might stand out in some way so he could use them to leave a trail. He wasn't going to sit here like a scared little boy for another moment. He was taking charge of this situation and if it meant instant death, then so be it! Better to die on his own terms than wait for death to come calling. As soon as he'd gathered enough markers, he was going in search of water and monsters, hopefully in that order.

***

Candy crept forward ever so slowly, using her elbows military style, careful not to make any noise that couldn't be attributed to the usual sounds of woodland animals. The movement hurt but she gritted her teeth and bore it, using it as a reminder that she didn't want David experiencing the same pain and it was up to her to prevent that.

She had the blanket that rolled up into a small bundle stuffed in one pocket, and an open can of the energy drink in one hand, having to be careful not to spill any as she crawled. She had an unwrapped cereal bar and two loose glucose tablets in another pocket.

Once they were organised, the three of them had moved back into close proximity to Andrew. Now, Candy went on further ahead as William and Jill watched from a short distance away. She'd made them promise not to come out of hiding if Andrew heard or spotted her too soon, made them promise to keep themselves safe to be there for David.

Eventually, she reached the tree that brought her as close to Andrew as she could get without being out in the open. She was pleased to find that it felt really close, closer than she'd thought. It gave her a little more hope that this would actually work. She hadn't told the others how much of a long shot she really thought this was.

Firstly, she poured some of the energy drink out onto the ground. The smell was strong, almost sickly. She paused when she saw Andrew lift his head and heard him sniff. She waited, holding her breath, trying to see if he would react further to the unusual aroma that had suddenly hit his nostrils. Seconds passed, then Andrew seemed to settle again as the smell faded a little. Changing tactics for now, not wanting to arouse his suspicion again, she took out the cereal bar, crumbling pieces of the soft, gooey, honey and yoghurt coated oats and chocolate chip pieces, throwing them so that they scattered silently around his back. The occasional one went too far and landed close to his sides, giving Candy palpitations, but he didn't seem to notice. Finally, she risked pouring out some more of the sticky liquid and pushing the leaves that it had covered closer towards him. She decided that was enough and sent up a silent prayer that this would work, and work in time, too. All she could do now was watch and wait.

***

David heard the stream before it came into his vision, the babbling and burbling instantly making his dry mouth salivate. Following the sound, he found it easily. It was crystal clear, the water sparkling, filtering itself over smooth rocks and a pebbly bed. It looked so good, and he was so very thirsty. This was it, the moment of truth. Time to decide.

He hunkered down and scooped his cupped hand through the water, loving the almost icy coolness of it on his skin. He brought it to his lips, millimetres away, already imagining how it was going to taste…so close…so thirsty. He couldn't even remember the last time he'd had a drink. He hadn't touched the sweet tea Mum had brought him at the hospital so that probably meant it had been at breakfast the day before. This was going to be so nice, so refreshing. He brought his hand closer still, puckering his lips to slurp.

He couldn't do it.

He wasn't brave enough to take the risk.

With a sigh, he dropped his hand, letting what was left of the water that hadn't ran through his fingers fall back into the stream, feeling massively let down both by the moment and himself. He couldn't help it, though. The water could save his life or kill him. There was an equal chance of both and those were odds he wasn't going to play with; he would just have to find a way home in order to survive. Now knowing what his final decision was, there wasn't any point in torturing himself by hanging around the stream. He might as well follow his markers back to where he thought the gate was located. He was about to rise when he heard a familiar chuffing sound. He looked around, seeing a Hoogle pointing at him with one talon, holding its tummy with the other. It was definitely laughing at him.

David didn't care. If he could see a Hoogle, then his Gatekeeper powers were working. He would be able to see the gate! He'd never been so pleased to encounter one of the snotty, ugly, scary little monsters. He grinned at it. "What have I done that's so funny this time?"

The Hoogle didn't answer, but instead, it loped over to the bank and plunged its long snout into the flow of the stream, drinking greedily. Having had its fill, it lifted its dripping snout and breathed out an open-mouthed 'ah' of satisfaction. Then it pointed at David.

"Me? You're telling me to drink?"

The Hoogle continued to point.

David was dubious. "I'm not so sure. It might be safe for you but that doesn't mean *I* can drink it."

The Hoogle cupped its clawed hand and scooped it through the water, mimicking what David had done earlier. It held it out towards David.

"You think it's safe?"

David didn't think the Hoogle understood the words but it must have picked up on the hesitance in his tone or uncertainty in his expression and body language. It nodded encouragingly, taking David's hand and pulling it down towards the water.

"Okay, if you think so."

He once more brought the water to his lips and this time, he drank.

***

Candy watched as ants carried off small pieces of oats. She could smell the sweetness in the air and it wasn't long before the flying insects she'd hoped for also sensed it and were attracted to it. She saw Andrew casually wave a hand in front of his face, the gesture lazy and unconcerned. Then he did it again, and again, then he was slapping at his neck and the waves of his hand were growing more frantic.

"What the heck! Go away, shoo!" Andrew exclaimed.

It was working! Candy could hear the increased buzzing and could make out the larger insects hovering around the spot where Andrew sat, trying to locate the source. Now Andrew was flapping both hands around, the gun waving frantically. If she left it any longer, he would be on his feet, and in her current state, she wouldn't be able to bring him down. Easing the blanket out and unrolling it, she made a dash for him, ignoring the pain to move as fast as she could. Before he knew what was happening, she'd reached him and brought the blanket down over his head.

"Hey! What's going on…gerrroffff me!"

Candy had no intention of getting off. In fact, she hung on for dear life as the blind Andrew tried to get to his feet. Then William and Jill were there, wrapping Jill's rope around Andrew. Candy jumped out of the way as they ran round and round, pinning the blanket in place and Andrew's arms to his sides. He still held the gun but couldn't raise his arm or see to aim it. The rope was tied tight, then Candy used the duct tape to bind his ankles before tipping him over onto his side. He looked like a giant, fleecy burrito. Ignoring his muffled yelling, Candy yanked the gun from his hand and ensured the safety was on before handing it to Jill. "Just in case."

Jill nodded and tucked it into the waistband of her jeans. "The Realm should be here eventually. I suppose until then we just have to wait. I'm hoping they bring a Gatekeeper so we know when the gate opens."

"Did someone mention that they needed a Gatekeeper?"

All three of them went wide-eyed, hardly able to believe their ears. They turned towards the voice.

"David!"

Jill reached him first, pulling him into her arms and squeezing him until he could hardly breathe. The others joined in, all three of them hugging him at once. "Oh, thank goodness you're okay. I've been so worried. I'm so glad you're back." Jill was saying through her happy, relieved tears.

"I'm glad to be home too, but maybe suffocating me when I've only been back for five minutes isn't the best of idea."

CHAPTER TWENTY-FIVE

"Knock knock, can I come in?"

"Sure you can," Candy said, smiling at how this time the roles were reversed.

Normally, it was David that was tucked up in bed after being wiped out by an adventure and her that was visiting. This time, it was she that needed to be put to bed to recover. She hadn't needed William's insistence, but she'd definitely needed Jill's help.

"I've brought you a cup of tea. How are you feeling?" David asked, sitting down very gently on the side of her bed, not feeling in the least bit uncomfortable with that, nor feeling the need to wait for an invitation. He handed her the mug of tea that Jill had insisted he take her.

"A bit sore but not too bad. That was some day, yesterday, for both of us," she said.

"It was, although I think it went worse for you than it did for me."

"I don't know about that. What was it like, David, through the gate I mean?"

They'd barely had a chance to chat. Shortly after David had reappeared back in his own world, the Realm had arrived, bringing with them the usual terse questions and bustling efficiency. Almost as soon as they'd arrived home, William had insisted on Candy having her wounds checked, clean dressings applied, and some serious rest. David had been left alone while they saw to her. This was the first chance he'd had to see her since his little solitary adventure.

"It was okay actually; at least that particular gate was anyway," David said. "You remember I told you it looked almost exactly the same on the other side?"

"Yes, I remember."

"Well, it pretty much stayed that way. I didn't see a single thing that doesn't exist here, no unusual animals, creatures, not even a plant or tree that looked different. Of course, I was there less than a full day and I didn't explore much."

"Obviously, you could breathe and stuff then or you wouldn't be back," Candy said, managing a grin.

"Yes, which was useful," he replied with a laugh. "But it was much more than that. Candy, it was amazing! I was so thirsty and I found a stream, but I was too scared to drink from it. What would you have done?"

"I guess I might have waited until I could feel dehydration setting in, then I'd have drank it anyway. Either that or just drank it straight away. Better to know one way or the other."

"That's exactly what I thought you'd do, what I was intending to do. But when it came down to it, I couldn't bring myself to do it. Not until a Hoogle appeared and told it me it was okay."

Candy sat up, wincing and almost spilling her tea. "It spoke to you?"

"Well, no, not in words. It kind of indicated that it was okay—body language, gestures, that kind of thing."

Candy leant back against the propped up pillows, wrapping her hands around her mug and looking thoughtful. "Oh, okay, not quite as shocking as I thought but still pretty amazing, right? It means they do have some of that con…cot…"

"Cognitive?"

"Yeah, that's it, thanks. Some of that cognitive intelligence you were talking about, doesn't it? I mean, it figured out you needed a drink but were afraid. That's a pretty high level of understanding, even smarter than a dog."

"Exactly! There's much more to the Hoogle than everyone keeps telling me. I have absolute proof of that now, and that was the best bit about going through a gate."

"What was the worst?"

"If it had been any of the other gates I'd seen, I would say encountering monsters on that side when you can't push them back and close the door behind them! That would be the obvious answer and the one I'd have given even if I'd never been through a gate. I didn't meet any monsters there, but even if I had it wouldn't change my answer. The very worst thing was thinking that maybe I didn't have my Gatekeeper abilities over there. I know I haven't had them very long, and I know I'm not that great with them yet and have masses to learn, but I felt absolutely devastated thinking that maybe I wasn't one. I don't know what I'd be if I wasn't a Gatekeeper. Does that make any sense?"

"I understand perfectly. I feel exactly the same way. I don't know who or what I'd be if I wasn't a Watcher. It's not just my job, or my calling; it's my destiny. It's everything I am and everything I'll ever be."

"It's so great to have someone to talk to who knows and feels the same."

"I hope I'll always be around to be that person."

"Me, too, because I've got something else I really need to talk about. Are you up for it?"

"I'm fine, go on."

"This has to be just between us, okay?"

Candy looked a little worried. "I can't absolutely promise that. I can maybe ninety percent promise, but if I really feel it's something William or Jill need to know, I'll have to tell them, but I wouldn't do that until we'd discussed it first. Is that good enough?"

"It'll have to be. I can't keep this to myself. You know how I've tried to use my compass around that gate and it always goes haywire but its fine everywhere else, and how Granddad said that a gate wouldn't affect a compass?"

"Yeah, but he said the Hoogle were just vermin so maybe the Realm don't know everything yet. Maybe gates affect compasses all the time but it just hasn't been noted or recorded."

"Could be, but it's only that one gate. It hadn't really occurred to me before but this highlighted it for me. Anyway, it was doing exactly the same on the other side of the gate. Not only that, but I checked it at the stream. I was quite a bit away from the actual gate then and you know we didn't have to go far away from it on this side before it settled down. It was still doing it. I watched from then on. It did it the entire time I was on the other side."

"I don't know if I would consider that weird, though. They might *think* they know lots about those other worlds, but I'm not so sure, and they admit they haven't a clue about the gates. Maybe nothing from our world would work on the other side."

"I'll admit that's a good point. In fact, your phone wouldn't. I don't think that's it, though, not the whole story. While I was over there, I fell asleep and I dreamt about Billie. I heard her calling for me, saying she was lost, asking me to help her, to find her. When I woke up, it stayed with me. It was so real, Candy, as if I'd genuinely, actually heard her. I've tried to tell myself it wasn't real but it keeps coming back to me. I can't get it out of my head."

Sympathy flashed across Candy's face. "That's not surprising either. She was your best friend. Of course, she comes to mind all the time and you think you see or hear her. You don't have any closure so your brain is always going to be questioning it and doubting if it's real."

"What you're saying makes sense but it doesn't feel right to me. I'm sure there's more. Did I ever tell you Billie had a matching compass with the same inscription? And the night she gave me mine, she said they were like that so that we would always find one another."

"No, I didn't know that, but then again, you two weren't my biggest fans at the time."

David turned a faint shade of pink. "Sorry."

"Water under the bridge, forget it. So you think that the way the compass acts has something to do with Billie?"

"I think so. I think that's what my dream was trying to tell me, too. There has to be something to it, right?"

"I can see you've thought a lot about it, but you're not telling me everything yet. What is it?" Candy suspiciously asked.

"Candy, I think Billie went through a gate, and not just any gate. I think she's in the world just beyond the Hoogle tree."

Once more, Candy almost spilled her tea in her hurry to sit up. "Promise me you won't go back through there!"

"I can't! I'm sorry but I can't make that promise. I have to look for her! If she's really there, she'll never find her way back without a Gatekeeper and she's in such danger from so many things."

"But you don't even know if she is there. You could put yourself in the same danger for nothing."

"It makes sense, though, doesn't it? I told Candy about the creatures I'd seen, then I told her about the gates and being a Gatekeeper. She packed her backpack and went off alone into the woods. You know what a daredevil she is!" David was almost pleading now. "Now that I've put the pieces together, I'd bet my life she went deliberately looking for a gate and stumbled through one. Now she can't get back. It would explain why there wasn't a single trace of her and how she disappeared so quickly and suddenly without saying a word to anyone, not even me. She likely thought she'd be back in a few hours and no one would have to know."

A pained expression crossed Candy's face. "How could you? You know telling anyone is forbidden and it's that way for a reason. The more someone knows, the more curious they get, so the more danger they're in, and the more reasons Seekers have to come for them."

David hung his head. "I understand that now, didn't really grasp it at the time."

"Well, what's done is done, I suppose, you know better now. It does raise questions about Billie, though. What you're saying sounds as if it could be right."

"So you agree?"

"I suppose it's possible, but you can't go back there, you just can't."

"I have to. It's Billie."

"Then we'll go to the Realm with our thoughts and let them handle it."

"You know they'd only shut down the gate. They wouldn't care about sacrificing one stupid girl for their bigger cause of saving all of humanity. They'd close it and leave her there to die. You also have to think of the Hoogle. They rely on that gate opening frequently for food. Then there's the fact that I'm the one who told her. I'd be punished, and I have no idea what that punishment might be. They might take away my Gatekeeper status."

Candy was silent for what felt like a lifetime to David. He wondered if she was going to make good on her threat of going to William or Jill. If she did, they'd likely keep him under lock and key forevermore.

Finally, she let out a bone-weary sigh. "You don't have to put me in difficult situations. You're right; I can't go to the Realm. I won't have Billie or the Hoogle on my conscience. I don't feel right about keeping this from William either, though. That's just wrong."

"If you tell my parents, they might go to the Realm themselves, or they'd probably tell Granddad, and he'd *definitely* go to them. You'd still be condemning us all."

"Oh, God, David, you're right again. This just isn't fair. Let me think." She was quiet again but for a shorter time. "Okay, listen up. We'll make a deal. Once I'm better, we can really look into it then, together, as a team."

"You really want to help?"

"Course I do. I'd do anything for you to have your best friend back, David. We'll make it a priority once I'm fully on my feet, but only if you absolutely promise me you'll wait for me and won't go there alone."

David leant forward and gave her a very tentative hug, trying to avoid both her injury and her tea. "I promise. I think if we ever do find Billie, I'll have two best friends. You're the greatest Watcher ever, Candy, the absolute greatest!"

"Yeah, I know. Now go on, get out of here. You've scared, worried, and exhausted me enough for one day."

"Sorry, I'll let you get some rest. Sleep well."

"Goodnight, David. Sweet dreams."

"Sweet dreams, Candy. Get well soon. We've got so much to do."

"Don't I know it," she muttered, having already laid down her mug and snuggled down into her pillows. "That's what I'm afraid of."

David smiled and closed the door, knowing she didn't mean it. She loved this life as much as he did, and it was still only just the beginning for them.

About the Author

Den JR Hedges was born and bred in Hatfield in Hertfordshire, England. He is the oldest of three children to his parents Dennis and Helen. He also has a half sister and brother.

He married in 1985 at the age of 20, and his first son was born later that year. His marriage lasted for 11 years and resulted in his three sons Richerd, Matthew, and Alex (who are his world).

After various failed relationships, he ended up in Peterborough, England, where he now lives with his future wife, Jane. He also has gained three great step children from Jane in Michele, Kasida, and Ethan. He is now a granddad. He is very family orientated and loves nothing more than a nice family time.

The Gatekeeper and the Hoogle was an idea he had when he was at school in 1980, and although he started the story many times, it was never completed. He made a vow that by the time he was 52 he would have the book finished, which he did. He loved writing the book and he hopes you enjoy reading it.

Remember, the next time you can't find your keys, it may be the Hoogle!

Available Now:

THE GATEKEEPER AND THE HOOGLE

Coming Soon:

THE GATEKEEPER AND THE MISSING

Printed in Great Britain
by Amazon